VEN

'*I need you. I hope that something will make you change your mind and stay in Venice,*' the charming doctor Pietro Bassano tells Nurse Theresa Callan. But can she ever be satisfied with a relationship that ends at the door of the operating theatre?

VENETIAN DOCTOR

BY
ELSPETH O'BRIEN

MILLS & BOON LIMITED
London · Sydney · Toronto

First published in Great Britain 1983
by Mills & Boon Limited, 15–16 Brook's Mews,
London W1A 1DR

© Elspeth O'Brien 1983

Australian copyright 1983
Philippine copyright 1983

ISBN 0 263 74443 4

Set in 11 on 12½ pt Linotron Times
03/1083–47,000

Photoset by Rowland Phototypesetting Ltd
Bury St Edmunds, Suffolk
Made and printed in Great Britain by
Richard Clay (The Chaucer Press) Ltd
Bungay, Suffolk

CHAPTER ONE

'Sure you can cope with the next case?' Nurse Harding looked down at the shaking shoulders of her friend who should at that moment have been scrubbing up for the second case of the long day.

'Of course. Is the patient up already?' Nurse Theresa Callan dashed away her tears and put back her mask. 'I'm fine. It's just that suddenly I realised how much I was going to miss you all.'

'Oh, is that all it is? You'll forget us and the theatre as soon as you start midder. I thought perhaps you were upset by that lovely man who came in to watch the last open-heart surgery.'

'Why should you think anything of the kind?' A kind of self-protective annoyance made her speak more sharply than she intended.

'Oh, it's just that he saw you in here and sent me along to see if you were all right.' Theresa blushed. 'He seemed quite concerned.'

'Concerned because he thought I was upset, or because he was wondering who would scrub for the next one?' Theresa gave a short laugh. 'He's got it all wrong, but what does it matter. He's here to watch and to learn I suppose, and we'll see his back before the afternoon is over.'

Staff Nurse Callan turned her thoughts to her work and followed Nurse Harding into the scrubbing bay where Mr Nuttall, the world famous authority on surgical procedures on the heart and lungs, was talking to the registrar and a man in a mask and cap who seemed about to join the team for the next case. Theresa's heart sank. He was still there. She glanced at him again, reluctantly aware of his fine brown chest and the taut muscles of his shoulders and throat. Mr Nuttall nodded and she turned away to the scrubbing bay, paying scrupulous attention to the cleansing process that would prepare her for the gruelling hours ahead. Her gloves slicked over her powdered hands, and the gown, for once, was almost her size, when it was hitched up slightly at the waist by the nurse tying the cord. It only just brushed the white theatre boots that were a rule of theatre.

Resolutely, she ignored the brown eyes that looked at her so boldly over the mask and soon there was no time to think of him. She had three trolleys, laid up with an assortment of instruments that to the lay person might seem an odd collection of unrelated items, but to the nurse or theatre sister assisting, made a lot of sense. Theresa knew that as soon as the patient was in position on the table, and the skin had been purified with the antiseptic dye in a spirit solution, she would be expected to know which instruments to hand, which swabs to use and what apparatus might be needed to suck away fluid and blood, to seal bleeding points and to make each stage of the operation as smooth as possible for the surgeon.

For the first half hour, hardly a word was exchanged. It was only when the ribs were exposed and the decision to resect two of them had been taken, that there was a discussion between the surgeon and the stranger, who seemed to know all about it, to Theresa's chagrin, asking very searching questions. Mr Nuttall seemed delighted to share his knowledge and more than once stressed the importance of teamwork for such difficult cases. 'Wednesday and Friday won't be the same when we lose Nurse Callan,' he said. 'I like her to scrub for me for the big things but I shall have to be at the mercy of whoever takes her place.'

Oh, please, don't start that all over again, thought Theresa. During the first case, Mr Nuttall had waxed almost sentimental about her leaving St Edmund's and there had been murmurs of agreement from the rest of the staff. While they were talking, the tall man with dark eyes had come in, waiting well back from the operating table until he was noticed by Sister and his presence was brought to the surgeon's notice. He had missed a lot of the conversation but was just in time to hear a part of it. 'I shall do some private nursing until I go to Queen Charlotte's in three months' time,' Theresa had said, 'but I can't say I feel very happy about it. The woman I was going to nurse has decided to postpone her operation and as it isn't really urgent, her doctor can't insist that she keeps to a schedule, so now I have to go to Italy to nurse an Englishman who is staying at a luxury hotel.'

'Know anything about him?' said Mr Nuttall. 'He's lucky to have you going out there.'

It was at that moment that the stranger came into the theatre.

'I only know that he is called Sir Julian Speaker and he lives in the Danieli Hotel in Venice. He's a heart case—I expect I'll find he's a dyspeptic hypochondriac who only needs to eat plain food for a month and do a little work to make him quite well again.'

'You sound unimpressed by the prospect of a trip to one of the finest hotels in Venice,' Mr Nuttall was amused.

'I've never been to Italy, but one hears such stories about over-sexed Italians who harass lone women that I can't say I'm looking forward to it.'

Sister introduced the stranger, in a whisper that Theresa didn't catch, but to her shocked amazement, his eyes blazed at her as if he wished her some harm. She turned back to her trolley, confused by the intensity of his stare.

'If you mean the Sir Julian I know, you wouldn't dare to speak of him like that.' The voice was icy, but controlled, and was for her ears only as he bent as if to inspect the instruments on the Mayo table that had just come from the steriliser for the next stage of the operation. She glanced up and then back to the table as Mr Nuttall wanted a swab on a long handled holder. 'He has done much to help

Venice in the restoration of her heritage, alerting his own blind and insensitive nation to the need for money and skilled care before it is lost for ever! He is also,' he continued relentlessly, 'one of the finest men I have met, and very ill. He is not, as you seem to think, a dilettante tax-dodger with more money than sense, and I think, Nurse, that he deserves better than you.'

The second case finished, with the stranger who everyone addressed as Peter, scrubbing and taking over the closing up of the chest wall and the skin. In silence, Nurse Callan handed him everything he needed and took a grim pleasure in knowing that it was impossible for him to fault her. As he stood back from the neatly closed incision, he wiped the surrounding area with care, throwing the last swab on to the pile where the swab count had been completed before the deep wound was closed.

Mr Nuttall came from the surgeons' room wearing his dark suit. 'Would you mind going down with him, Peter? I have to see a patient in the Wing and I'm a bit later than I thought I'd be. Come to dinner tonight.'

'I'll go to Recovery for you,' he said, 'but I'm afraid I can't eat with you tonight. I have to get back and cope with a very sick man who I think has left it too late for my help.'

Mr Nuttall waved his thanks to the theatre staff as they left the theatre and the house surgeon strapped on the dressing while a nurse made sure that every trace of blood was cleaned from the patient's skin and put on a clean gown before he went back to the recovery ward to be watched and carefully monitored for the next few hours.

When Theresa came back to the theatre after pushing the last trolley into the sterilising room for cleaning and re-packing, the medical staff had gone, leaving the usual trail of discarded garments on the floor. She picked up a mask and put it with the other soiled laundry. I didn't see his face, she thought. She shuddered, slightly. That voice— smooth and quite cold. It was quiet and yet the impact of his words had been like a blow in the face, an insult to make her feel that she was a thought- less, ignorant woman unworthy to be considered as a suitable nurse for this paragon who could make the dark stranger erupt into such a show of protec- tive anger. He *is* dark, I suppose? she thought. Some men have brown eyes and fair hair but his skin was dark too. No blond could have those dark fingers and such jasper-dark eyes. She ran the tap over the instruments impatiently, making the water spurt out over her gown. What did it matter what colour his eyes were, or his hair? She smiled. He was probably completely bald, with warts and a thin hard mouth.

'So, you really are leaving us, Terry.' The anaes- thetist had come back to collect his case of air-ways and odd valves, lubricants and phials of in- travenous drugs which he carried with him to each hospital and private nursing home he visited, not trusting any theatre to have exactly what he needed, but hardly ever having to open the case. He smiled and his tired, kind eyes showed real concern. 'We'll miss you, you know.'

'Don't,' she said, the tears welling up again. 'Everyone has been so sweet to me here. I must be mad to leave.'

'You can come back when you finish midder and find that babies bore you, or you can attach yourself to a clinic and have as much work as you want. Just give me a ring if you ever need that kind of work.' He chuckled. 'Our Pietro seemed a bit put out.'

'Who?' She frowned. 'Why do you call him that? Mr Nuttall call him Peter and so did you in the theatre.'

Ben Mather grinned. 'Don't you think he looks like one of those bottom-pinching Italians you were so scathing about?'

'He isn't!'

He shrugged. 'Stranger things have happened,' was all he would say and she relaxed.

'You had me worried for a minute,' she said. 'But he speaks such perfect English, he couldn't be anything else, could he?'

'Goodbye, Terry. See you,' he said and kissed her on the cheek. 'Be good in Venice and keep away from dark handsome men in gondolas.'

'I shan't have time to meet any,' she said, and packed away the respirator and suction apparatus.

'Come and have tea,' called Sister Pomery. 'I have the operation book to complete but you pour and have yours before you go. Nurse will clear the rest. You've been on your feet for hours.' She sighed. 'You'll be missed, Callan. It's selfish of me to say it, but couldn't you put off midder for another year until we've trained up at least two more good nurses?'

'I can't. I've accepted the course and you know how difficult it is to get in to the more famous places. I might come back later, if you'll have me, but I know I ought to get a few more qualifications if I'm to continue in this career.' She sipped her tea and Sister Pomery wondered how a girl as pretty as Theresa Callan had kept free of marriage or at least a firm relationship with one of the many men who found her attractive. The auburn hair lay damply on the pale brow and the huge green eyes were sad but very beautiful.

'I envy you Venice.' Sister Pomery sighed. 'It's ages since I went abroad for a holiday and Venice is my favourite place.'

Theresa saw the fleeting sadness in her eyes and wondered if Venice had been the last place that Sister had visited with her husband before his death. 'I'll bring you back a souvenir,' she said lightly. 'I don't think I can manage a gondola but maybe a gondolier's hat.'

'Just have a good time and be careful. There is a magic about water, and, in my opinion, any city with canals should be banned to anyone who is alone and not already in love. You, with that mane of wonderful hair, will attract a lot of attention.'

'I can look after myself. I've heard so much about

Italian men that I shall probably be too careful and brush off even the most harmless of them.'

'You made quite an impression on our visitor today. He was very impressed by your work. He asked me all about you and about your training, and wanted to know why you were leaving.'

Theresa said nothing. It was her last day in the theatre and there was no point in telling Sister of the vibrant current of dislike she had caused by her casual remarks about a man she had never seen. He must have been trying to find out something that could be used against her to prevent her nursing his friend. If, as he said, Sir Julian deserved better than she, he would want to make it impossible for her to take up her post in the Danieli. 'Mr Nuttall said that the Danieli is a luxury hotel. I had no idea,' she said, to change the subject.

'It's right on the waterfront by St Mark's Square. Not on the square itself but to one side of what they call the Piazzetta, and it looks out on St Mark's Docks. It has a mention in many of the old books on Venice. Once, the water came up to the steps of the hotel. Now, the water taxi stops by the sea wall and luggage is carried the few yards across to the hotel.'

'Did you stay there?'

'For one blissful weekend,' Sister Pomery smiled. 'It was unforgettable. How long will you be with Sir Julian? It was all arranged in rather a hurry, wasn't it?'

'I have been paid a month's salary in advance and was told that I would have a room in the suite he uses.' She wrinkled her nose. 'It was rather odd. The secretary rang to say that their client, Sir Julian, had made it clear that whatever happened, I was to have the salary and the use of the room for that month if I wanted it.'

'Perhaps,' said Sister, slowly, 'they wanted to be fair to you. It's a long way to send a nurse if her job suddenly packs up after a week when she has been hired for a month and can't make any other arrangements. Is he so ill that he might die? Have you thought of that?'

'It could mean anything. He has a heart condition and is probably more acutely ill than the agency led me to expect.' Theresa bit her lip. 'I shall have to be prepared for a few shocks.' And now she knew that Sir Julian was really very ill, there might well be shocks, long hours of nursing and hard work. 'I'll finish drying the instruments and get them packed for sterilising, Sister. You have a thorocoplasty on Friday and the Aortic valve after the weekend, so I'll label the drums accordingly in case some bright nurse opens one for something minor.'

'Bless you. I won't say no. I can't think how we'll manage. Confidentially, I'd rather supervise theatre than scrub, and Mr Nuttall likes it that way.'

'Nurse Johns will do fine once I'm away. I remember being scared to show what I could do under the eagle eyes of my senior, but when she was off duty, I relaxed.'

Theresa finished her tea and went into the steamy instrument room. She wondered how she would react to a country she had never seen, in a luxury hotel, surrounded by people who spoke a language that was completely incomprehensible to her. I'll buy a dictionary and a phrase book at the airport, she decided. Peter was a very English name. That man must be British. Welshmen were often very dark, and some Scots. But Dr Mather had called him Pietro, in fun. She tried to forget the dark eyes that had reduced her to a jelly. Ben Mather was teasing, trying to convince her that he was Italian because he had heard a snatch of what the doctor had said. It was just the kind of thing he'd do. She closed the last drum and patted it. It was the last thing she could do for the old place and it was a labour of love. Her training had been happy and full of interest and when she found that her main skill lay in the operating theatre, she had been content almost to the point of getting into a permanent, comfortable rut that would lead no further for years, as Sister Pomery was young and needed her job since she had been widowed in a car accident.

The change to midwifery training had made sense and still did, but the three months before the course started must be filled with something that would pay the rent and feed her while she waited. Some girls could go home and live with families between jobs, but Theresa had only one aunt in Australia, a cousin in America and no loving parents to scoop her up. It was at least five years since

her father had sent for her mother to join him in
Africa where he was working for the World Health
Authority. They had worked together and con-
tracted cholera and died within hours of each other,
leaving their only daughter to make her own way in
life. It had sealed her decision to be a nurse, making
her determined that some day she would be of some
use, as her parents had been.

Her eyes felt hot and tired. I want to do good and
then that horrible man comes along and says that
I'm not fit to nurse his friend, she thought miser-
ably. She walked slowly over to her room in the
hostel and looked out at the tall trees lining the
wide avenue of fine buildings. His friend was in
Venice and he had said that he was too busy to stay
to dinner with Mr Nuttall, pleading pressure of
work, so that indicated that he would be too busy in
England to visit his friend, however much he said
he cared about him. At least I shall be safe from
that icy voice making snide remarks about my
work, she thought.

The soft spring breeze was cool with undertones
of winter in the early dusk. There might be bad
weather in England for some time until the sun got
into its stride, but Venice would be warm even as
early in the year as April. Sister Pomery had been
very helpful, telling her what to take with her and
what to have sent to the flat she had in London
which had been the *pied-à-terre* used by her parents
and which she now kept for holidays and visits to
the city with other nurses. Her clothes seemed dull

and she wondered if she would be expected to appear out of uniform at all. Her patient might well be the kind of man who hated fuss and would ask her to change out of uniform if she had to take him out somewhere.

Theresa inspected her bank account. There was a lot more money there than she had imagined. A little cash from investments was put into her account from time to time and she had spent very little on clothes for the past year. The first stirrings of excitement surfaced. I ought to enjoy Venice, she thought. Am I so afraid of the unknown that I shall be unaware of the magic of a fresh city, fail to see the beauty that must be screaming to be noticed?

Next morning the sun shone more brightly than it had done for a long time, making Cheltenham a city of graceful mellowness and gentle views, so she went shopping, suddenly wanting to look good, wanting to make a good impression on her new employer and wanting to convince herself that she didn't care what one man with dark eyes thought of her. There'll be plenty of men who will look at me with pleasure, she thought defiantly, catching a glimpse of her good legs and bright hair as she passed the window of a department store. She did a double take and went into the shop. I have to begin somewhere, she thought. She went up on the smooth escalator and stepped on to the deep carpet of the dress department. One glance told her that this would be expensive, but there was no harm in looking.

To her relief, she was left alone to look along the rails and to select anything she wanted to try on. Two pretty skirts of heavy cotton became the basis of her plan and she picked out the colours that flooded one skirt and added light tops to tone. Her attention was caught by some beautifully cool cotton dresses, finely pleated, almost like the fabulous Fortuny dresses that had been fashionable when the Orient Express had had its heyday. She fingered one and let it drift back into its close pleats. It was a deep soft green and she knew that for her the cliché of green for redheads was true. She went back to it and caught her breath when she saw the price. For a cotton garment, she had never paid as much, but this was special. The salesgirl was close behind her, sensing her indecision. 'Try it on,' she said, and it was the soft voice of the temptress.

As she slipped the dress over her head, it had the feeling that it had come home. If she put it back on the rail and went away to look at other dresses, Theresa knew that each time she looked back, she would see a hint of green peeping out between the other garments, reproaching her for not buying. She went out and looked in a more distant long mirror and was both elated and shocked by what she saw. 'I couldn't wear it,' she began.

'It's fantastic,' said the girl, forgetting her smooth sales voice. 'It's really great, and you'd be mad not to have it. If I had a figure like that, I'd have it if it took the last penny I possessed.'

'It's too much. I didn't want to pay that for one dress. I'm going away for a month and I have other things to buy.'

The girl reached over and sighed. 'Oh, dear. Stay there a minute. I'll have to call my supervisor. Someone tried this on and tore one buttonhole. I'm glad it wasn't me who served her. You might get a good discount. We can't sell it as perfect like that.' It was as if she wanted Theresa to have it so badly that she was prepared to point out any fault that would lower the price. The buttonhole only needed five minutes' careful sewing with the right colour thread and it would be as new. She came back, smiling. 'Between you and me, we've had one or two who have put it on and found it showed every bulge. My supervisor had it marked down for the sale next week, and, to make sure it sells, she says you can have it sale price.'

'It's a conspiracy,' murmured Theresa. 'I'll take it. I may never have the chance to wear it but I love it.' She chuckled as she changed back into her jeans and shirt. It wouldn't do a heart case any good to see her like that, but on the other hand, it might be useful if she had to have an evening meal in public with him. She bought a silk shirt that would go with the pale blue cotton pedal-pushers or with one of the skirts, and a coffee-coloured silky dress with simple cap sleeves that could be dressed up, if necessary, with black accessories.

Still mildly hysterical over the amount of money she had spent, she had lunch in a hotel restaurant overlooking a lovely park. She ordered a glass of red wine to go with her beef and wondered if she was going slightly mad. People wandered in the sunshine and office workers made use of the park, strolling and eating sandwiches bought in the local bakery as if summer had come. Only their clothes gave away the fact that the air was still too cold for sitting for any length of time on the solid wooden benches and stone walls of the park. Shall I be able to sit out in the warm air and enjoy the passing scene in Venice as easily as in respectable Cheltenham? she wondered. There was a man with dark hair walking along the near path on the edge of the park. He was not lingering as if he had time to spare. He walked with his head proudly high, his long legs striding past the slowly moving groups and couples, taking no notice of the admiring glances of girls from the nearby offices.

Why think of the man in the theatre now? This man was a complete stranger who happened to pass her window. She had seen nothing but a brown body and a masked face, and he had been covered completely with a gown. The man in the park wore a lightweight suit, a little too thin for the chilly morning, but no topcoat, as if he didn't notice the cold. His shoes were highly polished and of the finest leather, the cut of suit and shoes saying one thing. So, he wears Italian clothes and handmade Italian shoes! she thought, resentfully. That doesn't link him with the man in the theatre. This is a tourist—or a businessman intent on getting to a business lunch. He has nothing to do with medicine.

At the zebra crossing, he paused and waited impatiently. He crossed and entered the hotel and Theresa lost sight of him. She glanced round but he didn't come into the restaurant and her curiosity was tinged with relief. It was stupid to see any connection. She ordered fruit salad and coffee and read a small book about Venice that Sister Pomery had given her. Once more she glanced up but he didn't appear. Her coffee finished, Theresa went out through the lobby where a pile of luggage sat waiting for collection. On one case, set apart from the others and leaning against a flight bag that was very much like the one carried by the man in the park, was an airline label to Italy.

It follows, she told herself, trying to be calm, that the man I saw in the park *is* Italian and naturally will go home. I have Italy on the brain just because that silly Ben Mather joked about it. The man from the theatre has gone back to his own long-suffering staff in another British hospital.

CHAPTER TWO

THE SUN reflected from the water was dazzling and the heat was almost too much after the flight from Gatwick. Theresa stood in the shade with her luggage at her feet and wondered why she had come. It had been better on the plane when she had something to take her mind from the work ahead. Perhaps once she was busy again the sensation of being marooned in a foreign country with no friends might lessen. She shielded her eyes and looked out over the water at the fast-disappearing motor launch belonging to the Cipriani Hotel. It all seemed impossible now, but, looking back, she was glad to have been of use.

As the slowly-moving crowd had made for the narrow gateway to the tarmac at Gatwick, a large man with a bag that was almost too bulky to place under a seat on the plane had pushed forward, making several people look at him and mutter about people taking their places in the queue. A slightly-built woman had slipped and her high heel caught the metal edge to the floor-covering trim. Theresa bent forward but wasn't in time to stop her falling, and the next moment all was confusion. The man pushed forward, pretending it had nothing to do with him, even when the back of his neck was red with embarrassment. The woman collapsed on the floor, her face contorted with pain. A swift glance showed a rapidly swelling ankle and Theresa was left at the back of the line with the injured woman. A girl in the uniform of the airline came quickly, obviously worried.

'I have to get to Venice,' the woman said, through gritted teeth. 'No, I can't come to the emergency lounge. I have to get on that plane.' She looked up at Theresa. 'You are due to leave, also?' Theresa nodded. 'If you can help me on and off the plane, I shall be fine.' Her pallor belied her words, but she struggled to get up.

'Is there a wheelchair?' asked Theresa, briskly. 'I have to get that plane, too. If you can get us on board, supply me with a good crêpe bandage, some ice and some towels, I can manage. I have seen this happen before,' she said, instinctively unwilling to make the announcement that she was a professional nurse.

'Are you sure?' The girl was relieved. She raised the phone and asked a question. 'Chair along in two minutes. I'll get the first-aid things and tell them on the plane to make room for you together. Someone will have to move if you aren't sitting together. Better be in Club Class. She glanced at the injured woman's ticket. 'I see you are already booked in there and there are several seats free.' She smiled at Theresa. 'The least we can do is to give you the same facilities if you do our job for us, the staff are very busy on short runs and haven't time for individual customers.'

In a few minutes, they were going out to the waiting aircraft and now empty steps that loomed high above them. Two men appeared to help, lifting the woman easily up to her seat and depositing her with care. Theresa followed, the crêpe bandage in her hand, and the airline girl came after with the expensive hand luggage, a tray of ice and some towels. In the area curtained off for Club Class passengers there were few people, and a lot more privacy than in the main cabin. Theresa waited until the order to fasten seat belts was cancelled, then began to work in unhurried concentration. First she put ice in tissue and laid it on the swollen ankle, feeling around gently to make sure that as far as she could tell there was no fracture, then she bandaged the ankle firmly and comfortably to give support.

'That's wonderful.' The colour was coming back into her face and Theresa saw that her patient was a very elegant woman with high cheekbones and aristocratic wrists. She was slim and very light, which accounted for the ease with which she had been lifted into her seat, and she was very grateful. 'You have the magic touch and now I can face the journey. I was very anxious to get to Venice as I have a dear friend who is ill there. I shall go to the Cipriani today and visit him tomorrow.' Her glance took in the simple cotton jeans and inexpensive tee-shirt that Theresa wore for the journey. 'Where are you staying? At the Lido?'

Theresa had no idea where the Lido was, but knew from the tone that it was not as smart or as costly as the Cipriani. Her Irish pride flared. 'I'm staying at the Danieli,' she said, omitting any reference to working there, or to the fact that she was a nurse.

'Really?' The well-tended eyebrows were raised and she smiled. 'I shall call in at the hotel tomorrow. Would it be a terrible imposition if I asked you to be there to help me from the launch and take me into the hotel? I shall bring a walking cane or a long umbrella to help me, and, if necessary, I can borrow a wheelchair from the hotel, and there is always *uno ragazzo* to push me in the chair.' She laughed and her face became beautiful in the way of Italian women, switching from serenity or seriousness to sudden warmth. She sensed the question. 'I am half Italian, half English,' she said, 'I live mostly in London but I have many connections and some dear friends here.'

The journey was soon over and her ankle seemed to be less swollen when one of the ground staff came to help them down the steps. At the airport, most of the package holiday-makers were shepherded into waiting water taxis with their various couriers. Only Theresa, her patient and two others for the Danieli were left and no further confidences were forthcoming. The launch from the Cipriani Hotel arrived and a hand was laid on Theresa's arm. 'Remember, I am Francesca Vidali and I look forward to seeing you at ten tomorrow morning unless I telephone. *Le sono molto grato.*'

'That means she is very grateful,' said one of the others. 'You certainly did help her.'

Another water taxi tied up at the landing stage and someone called 'Danieli', Theresa's luggage was hauled on board and stacked with the rest against the over-hot plastic upholstery and the three passengers thankfully sank into seats under the awning. The boatman was dark and for a fleeting moment, she recalled the man with dark eyes who she most wanted to forget. If I have to see hundreds of Italians and they all remind me of him, I'm in for a rather miserable time, she thought. I don't even know what he looks like without a mask. The man at the hotel could have been like him. The build and force of movement was the same, but there must be many men who resembled him. A man already on the water taxi had brown eyes that watched her with warm appraisal but she sat with eyes downcast to avoid meeting his gaze and was relieved when he got out at another hotel. His eyes were caressing, as if it was a habitual expression whenever he met an attractive woman, but he had made no approach and Theresa gained confidence in her ability to discourage unwanted attentions.

The taxi continued through the marked lanes of the lagoon and from a side turning under a small bridge, a black barge came slowly into the main stream. It was low in the water with dull paint that made it even more sombre, and the gilded lions and figures on the prow and superstructure did nothing to relieve the impression of solemnity. A cluster of bright flowers covered the hold cover and two men poled the barge across towards an island on the other side of the lagoon.

A small cloud came over the sun and Theresa shivered in the shimmering heat. The barge went slowly on its way and she saw that the island was walled and had a sky-line of odd shapes that couldn't be big enough for houses. More boats joined them as the larger canals were reached and she forgot the black barges in her wonder as she looked at Venice for the first time. Sister Pomery was right. It was breathtaking in its beauty.

A glimpse of St Mark's, and the boat stopped at the steps for the hotel. Luggage was seized and taken on a wheeled trolley into the hotel and the passengers followed. The coolness of the air-conditioning was balm to hot and weary faces. The curved reception desk lay to the right and the two others were already receiving keys. Theresa was reluctant to approach the desk, knowing that once she did so, she was committed to meeting her patient. I am free for five more minutes, she thought, then smiled. What was there to make her anxious? Even if the staff spoke little English, she had a British patient who needed her care, and she would prove that she was not an unworthy person to care for him, whatever that rude man might think!

'I am expected in Suite 27a,' she said. 'Sir Julian Speaker?'

'*Momento*,' the man looked blank and retired to the back of the desk where he spoke to another man. They both regarded her with faint apprehension, as if she might prove difficult and was really not booked into the hotel. The first man came back. 'Will you wait, Signorina? I will ask.' He led her to a comfortable chair facing a window and left her. After ten minutes, she became uneasy. She found the letter from the agency and a letter from Sir Julian, signed by his secretary, who seemed to be a man, from the scrawled signature. She tried to read the name but gave up the attempt. She went back to the desk. The man was talking to a newcomer who listened and nodded his head as if making a decision. Keys dangled from his fingers as he turned towards her. The reception clerk smiled and turned away as if he had successfully passed on a troublemaker to another more capable mind.

'Come with me.'

Theresa stared. His face was expressionless but his eyes were the ones that had haunted her waking thoughts ever since she saw them over the theatre mask.

'You wanted to go up to the suite, so what are we waiting for?'

'Who are you?' she said.

He smiled briefly. 'I had no idea that a white mask hid so much. You *do* know that we have met? And where? What more do you need? Some proof of my integrity?'

'All I know is that I have come here to nurse Sir

Julian Speaker. I have no idea who you are apart from knowing that you can sew up an incision.'

He led her into a quiet waiting room at one side of the lift. 'Don't be alarmed,' he said, mocking her. 'I have no intention of attacking you.' He bowed slightly. 'I am Signor Pietro Bassano, surgeon in diseases of the chest and a good friend of Sir Julian's. I came here to assess him for surgery.' He looked at her sadly. 'Urgent surgery, which he has refused to consider for years. I arrived yesterday but it was too late. Our patient died this morning.'

'Oh, *no*!'

'Oh, yes.' His smile was bitter. 'The world is less of a place without him. The funeral will be in two days' time, after the autopsy report, which is being done for legal purposes and for the sake of science. Just as he wanted it.' He turned to the door. 'Shall we go up now? I have a set of keys to the suite and so has Sir Julian's secretary and stepson.' He piled her luggage into the lift and she stood with one case between her and the man who had just turned her next few weeks of life into turmoil. He saw how she moved away from him in the confined space. 'It looks as if your journey has been wasted, Nurse Callan. We are both superfluous and can go home again. You will have plenty of time to prepare for your midwifery course, without upsetting a sick old man in his last days.'

'You are the most unpleasant man I've ever met,' she flared. 'Just because you came into the theatre in the middle of a conversation and took some things out of context, it doesn't give you the right to talk to a complete stranger like that.'

'A stranger? Surely not. We have met professionally and you gave me to understand that you know all about Italian men. Does that include those of us who are only half Italian?' He moved closer and the lift stopped, the doors automatically opening, but he ignored them.

'What I have been engaged to do here is no concern of yours. I have letters telling me that I can stay here for a month if I like, whatever happens.' It came out defiantly. The last thing she wanted was to stay here with this man checking everything she said or did, but she wanted to make it clear to him that she was aware that he had not engaged her and that it was not up to him to tell her what to do.

'You speak Italian?' She shook her head. 'You have friends in Venice? I can see that you expect every man you meet to be a threat to your virtue, if that is still intact,' he said.

'You beast. I don't have to stay here and listen to you.' She took a step towards the door but to her horror it slid closed, to go down again now that another finger had pressed a button on a lower floor. He stepped over her luggage and took her firmly in his arms. His mouth descended on hers and she could move no further away to escape. He lifted his head and his eyes were burning jasper.

'You expect us to behave like this, and it would be a pity to disappoint you. All Italians are amorous morons, are they not?'

The lift doors opened and his smile was enchanting as he made room for two Americans who looked mildly surprised to find the lift engaged. He insisted on taking them to their floor and Theresa fumed silently until they were out of the lift and walking towards the suite once used by Sir Julian. The Americans went first talking volubly about the charm and good looks of the Italian who had been so polite. Theresa saw them go with a sinking heart. Heavy velvet curtains covered one end of the corridor, the lift was a long way back and the stairs ran by the side of the lift. There was no escape if he forced her to kiss him again. And she knew, to her shame, that she couldn't hold back a response of which she now hoped he was unaware.

He stood by the closed door. 'Would you mind taking me to someone with whom I corresponded about this case?' she said, coldly. 'I must see whoever is responsible for Sir Julian's affairs. I have only your word that I am no longer needed. They may have other plans with which I can help while I stay in Venice.' She drew herself up tall. 'Even if I am not required, I doubt if I shall be refused a night's lodging and some food.'

'You are right, of course. Even I would not deny you those essentials.' His smile was less mocking and she began to wonder if the encounter in the lift had been a fantasy. 'That other remark you made—

if you were needed to help here, you would do so, if you wanted to stay?'

'Of course.' Theresa wondered if there was a Lady Speaker who might be infirm and in need of care and comfort over the next few trying days. 'Anything to help the family.'

'You should go home,' he said. 'I can think of many reasons for you going, but if you stay, I shall hold you to your word.'

'But you have nothing to do with it.'

'I have everything to do with it,' he said, firmly, turning the key in the lock. She heard him murmur, 'And this is one good reason why you should go home, Theresa.'

A man rose gracefully from a low seat by the window. The table before him was covered with neat piles of papers and folders and the dark jacket that matched his immaculate trousers lay across the back of a chair although the room was delightfully cool. He smiled and advanced towards them, smiling. 'You are Signorina Callan? The photograph sent to Sir Julian by the agency did not give any indication of such beauty.' He held her hand for just a fraction longer than courtesy required and for a second Theresa thought he was going to raise it to his lips, but he released her and said briskly, 'You will need tea.' He lifted the house phone and gave the order, but his soft gaze remained on her face and form. 'All English ladies need tea,' he said firmly. 'I am Luigi Ravenna, the stepson and secretary of the late Sir Julian Speaker.' He glanced at Signor Bassano and shrugged. 'I have said that so often this day that I go on repeating it. The press have not stopped talking about Julian and I think now that even I need English tea.' He paused. 'Unless you would rather have Campari? Wine, or coffee?'

'Tea is fine,' said Signor Bassano, and Theresa formed the opinion that Luigi Ravenna was trying to establish his control over events and his late stepfather's affairs. He asked about her journey and insisted that she go to her room to find her way around until tea arrived. 'In Italy, *un momento* often means five or ten minutes,' he said, with a smile that was impossible to ignore. She felt herself warming to his courtesy and his instinctive knowledge that a woman who had travelled all day in hot weather might need time to freshen up if she was to feel her best.

'Have I time for a quick shower?' she asked.

'Of course. I believe that English girls are quicker at their toilette than Italian girls, but you have such wonderful complexions that only a trace of cream is enough to restore you to full perfection.' He showed her the room that she was to use, with a bathroom across a tiny hallway.

A bit smooth but nice, she decided and hurried to find a creaseless dress in her smaller case. She chose a cotton tee-shirt and one of the softly flowered skirts, the gentle turquoise of the shirt making her eyes even greener than usual. Freshened, she went back to the sitting-room and found that tea had just arrived. The two men watched her pour, and she wondered if they reacted to her in the same way. Signor Pietro Bassano accepted his cup without a smile, stirring the lemon until he made a whirlpool in the tea and then forgetting to drink it.

Theresa sipped hers and was surprised to find that it was well made. Sister Pomery had warned her about bad continental tea, but then she was forgetting that life in a private suite in the Danieli might have perquisites lacking in a lesser establishment. The atmosphere was relaxed as Luigi told her of the days leading up to the death of Sir Julian. It was clear that his stepson held him in great esteem and even the dour man on her left seemed to give him credit for affection and care in those last days. On most matters they were in complete accord, but under it she had a feeling that Signor Pietro Bassano distrusted the other man in some way.

It became clear that Pietro Bassano was also a relative of the great man, which probably gave him a closer tie than Luigi's of stepson without blood relationship. It seemed unlikely that a surgeon as famous as Pietro Bassano, and Theresa had now had time to recall that he was the man who had pioneered a very tricky operation that had brought relief and hope to many seemingly incurable heart cases, would be involved in any disagreement over property or money. Pride or vanity would be his Achilles' heel, she decided. He couldn't forget her unfortunate remarks about his fellow countrymen and couldn't wait to see her disappear up the flight steps back to England. If only they could turn back the clock and start again with a smiling introduction and mutual love of their profession of healing.

She sensed that Luigi was restless. He hinted once or twice that the other man must have very many urgent matters that needed his attention, but Pietro Bassano suavely replied, 'What a pity you have to go to Verona tomorrow. I expect there are many urgent matters to sort out before you go.' Luigi hesitated, then gathered up his papers. 'I think you are wise,' said Pietro Bassano. 'The signorina will want to sit in here before dinner.' Silently, he watched Luigi take his papers into an end room and come back for his briefcase. 'I believe you have a desk in your room? Everything you need?' Luigi gave him a dirty look. 'By the way, Signorina Callan has offered to help me and so I think I may stay here tonight, as I would have done if the operation I have to perform was for Sir Julian and not for another patient with the same condition.'

'Help you? But I had no idea . . .'

'You didn't know that I was going to be the surgeon treating Sir Julian until we met again, but the routine will be the same as it was at St Edmund's.'

'You know each other?' The shocked disbelief on Luigi's face would have amused Theresa if she had felt like laughing, but her fury made her speechless. How dare this man calmly hint that they were old colleagues, if not good friends, whatever meaning was put on that phrase in Italy.

Luigi recovered his outer charm. 'I must go, but with great reluctance. I must make sure that Pietro does not bore you too much with shop talk.' He smiled. 'But I hope that you will be here for a long time and we shall have many opportunities to know each other better.'

'I hope so, too,' she said. At least he was attracted to her in a way that she could recognise, and deal with, if necessary. He would never force kisses on her unwilling lips, crush her in a tigerish embrace. She blushed, and it was not because Luigi gently kissed her finger tips in parting.

'I'm afraid that Signorina Callan will be leaving us soon,' the smooth voice said. 'She has other commitments in England and when I have no further use for her services, she will be free to return.'

Luigi seemed about to protest but thought better of it and left without another word.

'I shall go back when I please,' said Theresa and hated the pettish tone of her own voice.

'Of course. You will decide when to leave, after I have no further need of you.' The magnetic charge between them grew.

Her mouth was dry. 'You have no need of me.'

'We have work to do tomorrow. After all, you have been paid to work here for a month, I believe. Luigi was quick to make sure I knew the details. He thinks that you will live here in this suite for that

time and consider it a holiday as Sir Julian re-
quested.'

She relaxed. Bless Luigi for making it clear to
this obtuse man.

'However, Sir Julian thought of others and I
know that his dearest wish was to help humanity.
The reason he consented to the operation was
not that he had any illusions that it would cure him,
but that the experience would help others when
they had to endure it, with more hope of recovery.
He would want you to help me. You have something I want, Nurse Callan, and you owe it to Sir
Julian.'

Theresa blushed to the root of her hair. 'You
make me out to be a grasping female who thinks
only of her own free time. When will you believe
that I'm not like that and I do have feelings?'

'I believe you,' he said, but his eyes told her that
the feelings he recognised were the sensual responses to his embrace.

She ignored the implication. 'Tell me what you
need tomorrow, and I'll be ready when you are.'
She smiled slightly, thinking of the modern equipment in the theatre that she had left. 'Can they cope
with such cases? Or do you have to bring in outside
help to make it possible? Do you want me to lay up
first or do I just walk in and assist as a theatre
nurse? You were pleased to point out that I have no
Italian worth mentioning. I doubt if I shall make
myself understood.'

'You will do as you did for Mr Nuttall. That's all I

ask.' It was more of a request than an order. 'I shall tell you if I want more from you.'

She glanced at him sharply but couldn't read his eyes. It was a relief to be on this professional footing, but difficult not to sense more in his words than he intended. I'm becoming neurotic and soon I shall imagine that every man I meet is out to seduce me she thought.

'Now, I think we should find a place to eat. I suggest an early night after your long day.' Was he being thoughtful or was it merely that he needed a nurse with all her wits sharp and sensitive to whatever the case presented?

'I can eat here. There is no need to put yourself to any trouble for me, Signor Bassano.' It was difficult to say his name when she still thought of him as Peter. But here in Venice he had become wholly Italian, as if the flight had changed him in some subtle way. Even his voice was less British and when he spoke to Luigi, in English because she was with them, it was two Italians talking.

'I expect you to follow the wishes of my uncle, so the least I can do is to offer you the time and courtesy that he would also want you to have,' he said, gravely.

Well, that's the smoothest way I've ever been put in my place! she thought. He's very polite but he's making it clear that it is not of his choosing to have to entertain a woman he doesn't like, but he'll do it properly and hate every minute.

'I could have dinner here with Signor Ravenna.

After all, we are both employed by your uncle . . . did you say he was your uncle? I thought he was just a friend.' Stricken with misgivings, she regarded him with troubled eyes. 'I'm sorry,' she said. 'You must have been very worried about him.' It excused at least some of his rudeness.

His dark eyes were more friendly. 'He was my mother's brother. She married an Italian who introduced Sir Julian to Italy a long time ago and he never lost his love for the country.' He looked at her as if trying to read her thoughts. 'It's good to make people love one's country and to help it in whatever way they are able. He made Venice his care and Venice will never forget.'

The tension that she had experienced whenever he looked at her with more warmth was growing again. The telephone startled them and he put out a hand to take the call. Luigi appeared in the doorway, saw that he was too late and went back, leaving the door slightly open. The rapid flow of Italian, the polite listening and more rapid phrases made Theresa even more aware that, if left on her own, she would find it difficult to go anywhere except for the tourist shops and the main sights where most people spoke a little English, French and German in order to sell or to entertain.

'I am afraid that I may have to go out,' he said in a clear voice. 'The report of the autopsy is ready and there will be papers to sign, as the doctor responsible for Sir Julian during his last hours. Luigi?'

Luigi came into the room as if he had been

waiting for the call. 'Was that for me?' he said, innocently.

'Partly.' He spoke a few words in Italian, then said, 'Let's talk so that Signorina Callan can follow us. It concerns her too. The report is through. I have to sign papers and you must take them for the lawyers tomorrow, but there has to be a slight change of plan. The funeral will take place tomorrow at noon which means you can't go to Verona until four.' He frowned. 'I must get in touch with the clinic. It also means postponing my operation until later tomorrow. You will come to the funeral?' He glanced at Theresa.

'Of course. Even if I never met him, I have formed the opinion that he was a remarkable man and I'd like to pay him respect.'

Was it a glimmer of tenderness in the dark eyes? It was quickly gone as Luigi protested that he would have to sleep in Verona the following night if he went there so late.

'We all have to endure some inconvenience,' he said, dryly. 'I have to change my plans, my patient will have a few more hours of suspense and Nurse Callan will have to put off her sight-seeing.'

The telephone rang again. He raised his eyebrows. 'You didn't say that you had friends here.' He handed the receiver to Theresa. 'It's an outside call.' He bent over so that he could speak over her shoulder, his mouth brushing her cheek, but she couldn't decide whether it was intentional or not. He said something which she took to mean that the operator could connect the call and then stood back, leaving the subtle fragrance of his aftershave on the air.

'Hello,' she said, cautiously, quite sure that there had been a mistake. 'Oh, hello. How is the ankle?'

'It's very much better, thanks to you. I shall be coming to the Danieli at ten as I told you and it would give me a lot of pleasure if you could lunch with me there.'

'That's very kind, but I'm afraid that when I arrived here I had quite a shock. I came to nurse an Englishman.'

She got no further. 'Not Sir Julian Speaker?'

'Yes, that's right.'

'But he's the one I was telling you I have to see. How is the poor dear man. I'm longing to see him. Is he asleep now? Perhaps I could talk to him for just a moment?'

'Oh, dear. I have rather bad news for you.'

'What is it? A reporter?' Pietro Bassano snatched the telephone from her. 'Who is this?' he said. He listened and surprised pleasure mixed with sadness. 'My dear Francesca, I'm afraid you are too late. Julian died soon after I arrived to assess him for surgery.'

Theresa heard sobbing and her heart ached for the woman on the other end of the line. But some of the ache was for herself. The voice that spoke to Francesca Vidali was tender and affectionate, full of concern. It was something reserved for someone he loved and Theresa knew that she had no part of that true feeling. He wanted her as a nurse and if he could get her into bed, he would try. That would be all he needed of the nurse from England, but Francesca could sob a little and gain everything she wanted from him.

He told her that the funeral was during the morning and suggested that she joined him in one of the following barges with Luigi and Signorina Callan. His glance wandered over to Theresa as Francesca explained that she couldn't walk well because of her ankle. He nodded and Theresa wondered what Francesca was saying about her. At last he put down the telephone, but it rang again, immediately. He gave a sigh, but the call was brief.

'That was Reception. They need your passport for the records. I will leave it there when I go out.' He looked at the clock. 'And that must be now or they will have gone home. It's very late but a friend promised to get the report done as quickly as he could. The least I can do is collect it as soon as possible.' He hesitated. 'I think perhaps you should have dinner here after all.'

'I am tired,' she said. 'Is Francesca coming tomorrow?'

'I'm sorry. I forgot that the call was really for you, Florence Nightingale.' So, she had told him in glowing terms about the nurse who had cared for her! Theresa turned away, and Luigi was standing in the doorway.

'Are you coming with me, Luigi?' Pietro Bassano said.

'I have several telephone calls to make if the funeral is to be put forward. Many people will want to come and I will make a list of guests who can manage to come to lunch afterwards.'

'Well, make sure that the Signorina has everything she needs and then leave her in peace. I'm afraid it's going to be rather a long day tomorrow for a girl unused to the heat of a Venetian sirocco, so we must make sure that she is not overtired tonight.'

Was there a veiled order in the words? Luigi nodded and said that he would eat later in the restaurant downstairs.

Theresa unpacked and had just put away the last of her clothes neatly, and tidied the room, when she heard the chime of the door bell outside the suite. A waiter entered with a trolley of food for one, tastefully arranged on silver dishes and accompanied by half a bottle of white wine on ice and a bottle of *acqua minerale*, to drink alone or as a dilutant to the wine. She realised that she was hungry but could hear no sound from the rooms occupied by Luigi or Pietro Bassano, so there seemed to be no reason why she shouldn't eat her dinner alone. She wondered who had chosen the delicate food—Luigi on his way to make those calls from the main desk? Pietro Bassano?—or had he just carelessly left the choice to the headwaiter, telling him to give her whatever seemed suitable for a girl from England?

She began to eat, enjoying the variety and presentation of the food, but gradually her thoughts dwelt on more sombre matters. She saw again the black barges and now realised that these were the funeral barges that took the dead to the Island of St Michael, the cemetery of Venice.

The suite was luxurious but lacked the touches that would make it a home. She wondered if Pietro Bassano had a home of his own, or a wife. She pushed aside the rest of her fruit, losing her appetite. Perhaps Francesca, with all her delicate elegance, was the woman in his life. Her fluttering, helpless hands could ensnare a man more closely than a firmer grip of shared professional interest and more robust contacts. It was stupid to think of them. It was none of her business, she told herself.

She yawned and pushed the trolley into the tiny hall that lay between the rooms of the suite. The waiter would collect it sooner or later and there was no urgency to get rid of it. She went to her room and opened the window as she would have done at home. Her room, being one of the smaller of the suite, did not face the water. A gust of hot air came in and she quickly closed the window again, remembering that the rooms were air-conditioned and that outside everything was hot and heavy with the sirocco.

She yearned to walk by the water, to see the glint of the late sun over the gilded lions of San Marco, but she was too tired and too afraid to venture out alone. Her silk kimono was soft and cool, the peacocks across the back a ripple of glorious colour against a pale background. She brushed her hair and wondered what she should wear tomorrow. A funeral and an operation. What a mixture in one day. Should she appear in uniform as representing her profession? She arranged her white uniform dress on a hanger outside the cupboard door and put out white shoes. She turned at a slight sound at the outer door. Thinking it might be the waiter to take away the trolley, she opened the door, just enough to hear what it was. The door shut and she assumed that she was alone again.

The door of her room was pushed open slowly, and Luigi stood there holding a silver ice bucket and a shrouded bottle of sparkling white wine. 'I thought I might join you for dessert,' he said. She pulled her kimono more closely round her waist. 'You look very delectable. Were you waiting for me, *cara*?'

'No, I was getting ready for bed,' she began, and saw that his eyes were over-bright. 'Please go away, Signor. I have a busy day tomorrow and I have had enough to drink for one evening.'

'So beautiful, the English, and not cold.' He wagged a finger at her. 'I hear they are cold, but it is not so. Such skin, such eyes.'

'I will come out there. It is cooler,' she said, trying to smile. He turned and went back into the sitting-room and she thankfully locked her door behind him. His hands beat furiously on the thick wood and he shouted a string of Italian that she could only imagine was not very polite. A door opened and slammed and another voice came to her, with cold clarity and authority that sent Luigi into muttering, resentful acquiescence. A moment later, Pietro Bassano knocked on her door.

'Theresa?' She stood silently, waiting to see if he too tried to get in. 'Signorina Callan. I must speak to you. It is quite safe, I give you my word.'

Slowly, she opened the door, ready to run back or attack if he assaulted her. Her wide eyes were green and bright with rising temper and her breast heaved with suppressed fear. Pietro Bassano stood in the doorway and stared at her without entering the room.

'I'm all right,' she said.

'I had to know.' His glance wavered and he looked away as if he couldn't bear to see her. 'If you must look like that, you little fool, you have only yourself to blame if every male within miles tries to seduce you.'

'I thought I was alone,' she said.

He gave a short, bitter laugh. 'In a hotel suite with two men? I can't believe that anyone can be as ignorant as that.' His gaze caught the virginal white of the spotless uniform on the cupboard door. 'Do wear that tomorrow. You were right to prepare uniform. It is fitting. Wear it to the funeral and again to the clinic. I want everyone to know that you are here on duty.'

'The hotel knows that. Surely it can't be right to wear uniform to the clinic and then go into the operating theatre? It was forbidden at my training school.'

'Once there, you will change into a cotton garment that is cool and fresh for each case, under your gown.'

'Then why make me wear it on a water taxi?'

'There are such things as personal reputations to consider,' he said, coldly. 'Now, lock your door and keep it locked all night and at any time you are alone, looking like that.'

'And if someone wants to ask me something?'

'Talk through the door, but lock it. Do you hear me? Lock it and don't open it to anyone, least of all, *me*.' He slammed the door and she heard the echo of his words long after he had gone.

CHAPTER THREE

THE LAST of the flowers floated away as the dark barge disappeared into the tiny dock waiting to receive the coffin of Sir Julian Speaker. Many boats and gondolas lay off the shore, water lapping a requiem against the hulls. Small motor boats and elegant yachts had joined the cortège and even though Theresa Callan had never met the man she had come to Venice to nurse, she felt the tears welling up and her throat was full of emotion. Such love and respect from people of another country was touching and impressive. Pietro Bassano and Luigi Ravenna, being relatives and close associates, stood at the back of the flower-decked boat like dark handsome statues, silent and reverent as the barge made Sir Julian's last journey.

The guests turned back to the Danieli to eat and drink to his memory. In one way Theresa felt apart, as if she didn't belong, but her uniform gave her an entrée into the world that Sir Julian had been living in for so long.

Francesca, lovely in misty grey chiffon, was surrounded by men who proffered help whenever she needed to move an inch. The style with which she used the tiny lace-trimmed handkerchief was not an affectation and her genuine grief was plain to see.

She was helped into the lounge by two very willing men and Pietro Bassano hovered near her for long enough to make sure that she had a very dry Martini and a comfortable footstool.

Theresa made for the stairs, hoping to avoid attention if she went to her room that way. She was half way up to the next floor when she became aware that someone was behind her. She glanced back and saw that Luigi was following her. He caught up with her on the first landing and smiled as if there had been no hint of unpleasantness the evening before.

'I have papers to fetch before lunch and then I have to go to Verona to see the lawyers. Why not come with me?'

'I thought you knew. I have to work this afternoon. I have to assist Signor Bassano with a case he has in a private clinic.'

'That? It is not necessary. Come with me and I will show you one of the loveliest cities in the world.'

He unlocked the door of the suite and while he was taking the key from the rather awkward lock, she went quickly to her room and locked the door. He might seem normally friendly but she was taking no chances. He tapped on the door. 'Have you not forgiven me for being a little too pressing last night? I am sorry, cara. I only wish to know you better. Is that a sin?'

Ignoring his pleas, she changed from her uniform, unable to face the guests in the white tailored garment that labelled her as a nurse on duty. The coffee-coloured dress with a shiny black belt and black sandals seemed fitting and she brushed out her glowing hair from the neat French pleat that went with uniform. She went to the door and stopped. Outside, there was silence, but she had not heard the outer door open or close. Had Luigi gone, or would he be there waiting for her as soon as she appeared from her room? The bell chimed on the outer door. She heard voices—one was a woman's. She walked into the hallway and saw the frown on Luigi's face and the surprise of the maid who was talking to him.

'Signorina Callan?'

'Yes,' said Theresa.

The girl looked at Luigi with suspicion. 'Signor Bassano told me that you are now ready for lunch, *si*?'

Theresa smiled warmly. 'He didn't give me long to change, but I am ready,' she said, making sure that the maid knew that she had not been alone with Luigi for more than a few minutes.

The girl smiled and Theresa followed her through the open doorway. 'I thought you had left, Signorina,' said Luigi with an air of innocence. So that's what he was telling the maid when she asked for Signorina Callan! He had no papers in his hands as he followed the two women.

'Haven't you forgotten your papers? You were in a hurry to get them before lunch, weren't you?' said Theresa.

He went back, and she knew that she would have to watch her step with him.

The assembled company were now talking cheerfully as they drank their aperitifs. To her surprise, Pietro Bassano came to her with a Campari on ice. 'Everything all right?' he said. 'I was afraid you might be late, everyone is ready to go into the restaurant.' His gaze was cool and penetrating.

'I had to change. My dress was grubby after the dust of the landing stage,' she said. 'Thank you for sending someone to check up on me, but I assure you that I was aware of the time and I am a very punctual type.' She looked at the people sitting, talking and knew that they would not be ready to eat for at least another ten minutes.

'You might have . . . been lost,' he said. 'Francesca was asking for you.' He moved away and Theresa went over to the Italian woman and asked about her sprain. Francesca seemed in good spirits now that they were away from the outward signs of mourning.

'The swelling has nearly gone, as far as I can see through the bandage,' Theresa said.

'I am very lucky. You helped me so much and it interferes very little with my plans.' She gave a wicked laugh. 'I have all the handsome men taking care of me. Perhaps I shall say it is bad tomorrow and have even more attention.'

'I'll tell them you are quite better,' said Theresa with a smile. No wonder Pietro Bassano loved her. Her vivid colouring and fine bone structure made an elegant picture that any man would want to possess.

'I was speaking to Pietro. I told him how grateful I am for your help and he is to bring you out to the Cipriani to dinner tomorrow night.' She saw the doubt in the girl's eyes. 'You want to come? You have not other plans?'

'No, I shall enjoy seeing you again and I hear that the Cipriani is rather splendid.' She forced herself to speak with enthusiasm, but wondered how she could make excuses to stay away. She could imagine what had happened. Francesca would have laid one bird-like hand on the sleeve of the man she loved and suggested that it would be good to give the nice little nurse a night to remember. He couldn't refuse, and so would have to endure the company of someone he wanted to see only over a theatre mask and she would have to behave as if she liked him enough to dine with him.

Theresa couldn't remember the food she ate that lunch time. She sat between a man who had once stayed with a family in the Lake District and took it for granted that Theresa knew every stone there, and a man who imported works of art. Neither spoke very good English and she was ashamed to think that she knew so little Italian and could not start a real conversation. Francesca smiled with animation at Pietro Bassano who sat on her left and he bent his dark head to catch every word she spoke, the jasper eyes full of a humour that Theresa had only suspected might be there when he was in company he enjoyed. Luigi made his apologies early and left for Verona as the lunch seemed to be going on for hours.

Pietro Bassano glanced at his watch at the precise moment that Theresa was looking in his direction. He nodded towards the door and she rose from her seat, murmuring excuses to her neighbours. Outside the room, he went to the desk to ask them to order a water taxi. His case was ready but he seemed to be waiting for Theresa to make some move. 'You have five minutes in which to change into uniform,' he said.

'But surely, if I have to change once I get to the clinic, I can come like this?'

'You are on duty,' he said curtly. 'When you leave here with me you are my theatre nurse, and I wish everyone to know that.'

'I don't understand. The hotel staff know about me, and I know no one in Venice, so I just can't see . . .'

'If you go out of here with me alone in a taxi, you will be thought of as my mistress, a girl I have brought into the hotel to sleep in the same suite of rooms with me. Coupled with the fact that Luigi is also living in the same suite, the implications could be very harmful. I have no intention of any reputation suffering. Hurry up, the taxi will be at the steps and I will wait there.'

She fled to her room. At least there was no danger from Luigi for at least a day and a night. She found a fresh uniform and left the soiled one for laundering. Her hair seemed to have a will of its own and even after she had tied it back with a wide ribbon, tendrils of auburn curls escaped. She caught up her handbag and make-up in a small case. Even if I'm in uniform, there's no reason why I should look a mess after the case, she thought.

The water glinted silver and blue under the bright sunlight. The humid thundery heat had given way to freshness and warmth with a drying breeze across the canal. Pietro put out a stiff hand to help her down and then steadied her briefly and impersonally as she went down the steps and under the shade of the awning. Her case was added to his and the water taxi swirled away in a white stream of bubbles towards a side opening in the Grand Canal. It was a like surreal dream, to be in full uniform, riding the waters of Venice with a sombre and completely wonderful man who was so close that she could touch him and yet so far away from her that she wanted to cry.

The silence between them was more than she could bear. 'I still can't understand why you want me in uniform outside the clinic,' she said.

'In those clothes you are a nurse in an official capacity at the Danieli.'

'I was a nurse when I arrived, out of uniform, to nurse Sir Julian, so what makes it so different now?' She glanced at his set face. 'I only ask because I can't think that anyone would notice or care about me and any relationship I might have with anyone in the hotel. You will be gone soon, I expect, and so there will be no means of linking your name with mine.'

He looked directly at her for the first time. 'Your uniform is your protection from men who might think you were here on holiday for quite another purpose. To be seen with some men would give that impression.'

'You mean Luigi?'

He nodded. 'It has been known,' he said. 'Here we are.' His relief was evident and he busied himself with his instrument case even before the taxi was tied up. He stepped ashore and held out his hand for her once more. 'Please don't think that Luigi is an evil man. He is a very good secretary and has been a loyal friend to Sir Julian, but you have no right to come here looking as you do.'

'I had no choice,' she said, 'But you have a choice. I can go to a *pensione* for a holiday while I am in Venice and you need not see me again.'

'I have to see you.' Her heart beat faster. Did that mean he thought of her as more than just a nurse? 'I have to take you to see Francesca tomorrow,' he said, 'and we have work to do.'

The clinic was tucked away behind a high wall beyond the huge wrought iron gates leading to the canal landing stage. The wide courtyard was cool and colourful with potted plants and pink roses clambering over the soft red-brick walls. It all looked ancient and calm, and there was no way Theresa could imagine it contained anything as efficient as the theatre at St Edmund's. A broken stem of rambler roses lay on the flagstones and she picked it up and inhaled the faint scent. She turned back to the water and dropped the flowers into the canal. 'For Sir Julian,' she murmured, and the gesture fulfilled a need to give him flowers as she had had none to give during the funeral journey. She looked up, to find Pietro Bassano watching her with an expression of surprised gentleness in his eyes. She blushed and tried to laugh. 'Tidying up the courtyard,' she said.

She followed him into the hall and looked up at the carved wooden ceiling. This place was not a clinic! It was more like a very old and beautiful private house.

'It was once a fine palazzo with many servants and its own gondolas, with gondoliers in livery to match the trappings of the boats,' he said.

'Were those the colours on the poles out there?'

'Yes. Rose and silver and grey stripes, like very indigestible sugar candy.' It was said lightly but Theresa felt that he had something to do with the family who had lived there. 'Come, we are late. *Andiamo!*'

They went through a wide doorway and opened another door. Theresa gasped. A corridor of spotless white tiles stretched before them, the ceiling was a mass of hidden lights and there was no shelf or crevice that could harbour dust or germs. A white-coated man greeted them and, to her surprise, Theresa found that she was very much the centre of attention. A sly smile touched her lips as she saw that Pietro was less than pleased to have her welcomed so effusively.

'We send surgeons to learn new procedures and even when we explore our own methods, we are helpless without good back-up staff. Nurses may read a hundred books but one afternoon with such as you, dear Signorina, will teach them more,' the white-coated man said.

'You are too kind,' she murmured. 'I hope I can help, but you must remember that I speak no Italian and so may make mistakes.'

'That is not possible. Pietro has told me that you work so well together there is no need of words.' He laughed and his plump face shook with delight at his own wit. 'It is like love . . . it needs no words, *si*?'

'Your English is very good, but I can tell that you are a true Italian,' she said, with a wry smile. 'Where may I change?'

'The nurse will take you and *il dottore*.'

Theresa was guided along the corridor to a side-room where she was given a simple shift of white cotton, very fine and cool. It made sense, both as a hygienic precaution in hot weather and for comfort, and she thankfully slipped out of her uniform dress and into the fresh garment.

The theatre was modern and had the air of quiet efficiency that comes from good training and complete cleanliness. She relaxed. It wouldn't be as strange as she had imagined. The scrubbing bay was wide and well lit and when she turned to put on gloves, she found three pairs of various sizes from which to choose. She smiled as she selected the size she wore and when her gown was tied firmly, the trolleys were wheeled in with the many instruments still in the perforated stainless steel trays from the sterilisers. She knew it made sense to bring them in like that so that she could arrange them as she liked.

A nurse stood with pad and pen waiting and Theresa laid one trolley with all the skin preparation swab holders, the scalpels for the skin incisions and the first synthetic ties for bleeding points. She counted swabs for this trolley and put a given number on one side. The next trolley was laid with instruments used deeper in the muscle tissue, and the rib resectors and deep clamps and retractors. If this stage was kept separate, it was easy to make sure that nothing that had touched the skin could contaminate the sterile, deeper tissues. It also meant that one trolley could be whisked away at an early point in the operation to make way for the heavier, essential equipment. A bowl of instruments, ready to be put on the Mayo table high above the site of operation, was ready to be transferred as soon as the patient was on the table, the diathermy pad was fixed and the anaesthetist was happy for the case to begin.

Pietro came in, scrubbed and gowned, and looked at the trolley, grunting his approval.

'I hope I can help you,' said Theresa. 'If you need

anything not here, you will have to ask the staff. Remember, I speak no Italian.'

His eyes were dark and unfathomable. 'How often did you have to speak to Mr Nuttall? When he needed something, you handed it him, often before he knew that he needed it.' A hint of mockery lit the dark depths. 'There was a bond between you. I want that bond, Nurse Callan.'

She shivered. His eyes spoke of a bond that was too dangerous to imagine.

'The staff here—will they object to a stranger scrubbing for you and taking the place of the regular nurse?' she asked.

'They would rather learn so that I don't shout at them,' he said, complacently. 'And the men will envy me, thinking that you are more to me than just a theatre nurse.'

'And yet you made such a fuss about me looking professional! You *are* joking?'

'Of course, Nurse Callan. Many men may lust after your body. I want your skill.'

She turned away, not knowing if she was glad or insulted now that she knew for certain that he didn't want her as a woman. The patient was wheeled in, and in minutes, everything was ready. There was no time to think about possible personal slights. The theatre was tense with the feeling generated by an urgent case who might be given a better chance of living a normal life if his aortic valve was repaired or replaced by this much simpler method than many surgeons were using.

The first trolley was discarded and the growing rack of swabs showed that the surgeon was going deeper. Intravenous blood was started and a careful check kept on body temperature. The man in the sterile gown standing by her side, working swiftly and surely through every new stage of the operation, held out a hand, took what was given him and Theresa was always ready with the next instrument. The first hour went by, and then the next, but nobody was thinking about time except the anaesthetist, who had to keep the patient fully relaxed on the minimum of anaesthetic, holding him lightly between coma and consciousness.

A too-eager nurse came forward to look into the cavity when the heart was exposed and Theresa gasped. 'A fresh gown and I'll have to scrub again,' she said. 'The pen in her pocket caught my glove.' Pietro Bassano swore softly. 'It's all right,' said Theresa crisply. 'There are four swabs on holders, the diathermy is there and your house surgeon has the sucker.' She dashed away, peeling off her gown. The taps were fierce and a spray of water splashed her down the front of the fine cotton shift, making the fabric cling like a second skin. 'Can I have a plastic apron?' she called and Pietro Bassano called for one so that the dampness wouldn't come through the fresh sterile gown and be contaminated. He turned to see what was happening and saw her standing with her hands outstretched, ready to take the apron, her body outlined in beautiful clarity like a Greek goddess on a vase.

'Sorry about that,' she said, returning quickly once her gloves were on again.

'It was a pleasure,' said the doctor who had first greeted her, and a murmur of laughter made her blush.

The valve was working well, blood was running at the correct rate and the patient seemed better for their efforts.

'I want to close,' said the surgeon. 'Swabs?'

Theresa told him crisply the number she had and asked him to make sure they tallied with the ones on the board. The nurse stood by, nervously, but as soon as the total was correct, Theresa smiled. 'Would you tell her that she has been a great help to me, please,' she said, and had the pleasure of hearing the surgeon say so, a trifle unwillingly. The nurse smiled and seemed delighted.

'Now she won't be nervous the next time you come here and she will *never* again do what she did today,' Theresa said.

'What a wise head in that fiery hair,' he said.

'What now?' said Theresa as the last trolley was taken away and the patient taken down to the ward. A nurse stood by her side. 'Do you speak any English?' she ventured.

'I have come,' she said slowly, 'to make you bath in there.' She pointed to the side-room where Theresa had changed. 'Signor Bassano said to take you, and for coffee.'

The man in question came back from the surgeon's room wearing loose theatre trousers and a towel slung round his neck. His skin was smooth and sparkling with drops of water. Theresa looked down, afraid to trust her expression. 'You've time for a quick shower,' he said. 'I shall see the patient before leaving, so be ready at the gate in an hour with my bag packed ready. I've told them to clean my things first,' he said, as if his wish must have priority.

The pretty Italian nurse sighed. 'If I had not my Roberto, I would fall in love with *il dottore*. So handsome, such *maschio*!'

'Such arrogance,' said Theresa, shortly.

She was ready long before the hour was over and he seemed to expect her to be there by the water taxi even though he, too, was early.

'How is he?' she asked.

'I think he'll be fine.' He smiled, but it seemed forced. 'Thank you,' he said. 'Let's get on the water and have some air!'

Once more under the awning, with the breeze touching the damp tendrils of her hair, Theresa had time to be satisfied with the afternoon's work. Afternoon? She glanced at her watch.

'Yes, it is later than I intended, but I hope you are not tired.' She looked surprised. 'I know that surgeons seldom think that a nurse can be tired, but here you have extra pressures of heat and strangeness.'

'It wasn't strange. I enjoyed it,' she said, and was dazzled by a sudden smile. 'The clinic is beautiful, and how clever to keep the façade and courtyard so beautifully.'

'It was a lovely house a few generations back,' he said. 'My family owned it and left it when the war came. Now, it is mine and it is perhaps more useful than it was. I keep rooms there for my use, but it is a very well-run clinic and nursing home now.'

'If you have rooms there, why stay at a hotel?'

'I promised Sir Julian that I would stay while he was ill. I saw no reason to give up my room there when I knew that I had to stay for a while longer.'

'I suppose there must be lots of people wanting to know about Sir Julian. It would be a burden on the clinic to have to take all those calls,' she said.

'Something like that,' he said. 'But I have other responsibilities near the lions of San Marco,' he added, cryptically, 'and business to attend to with Luigi.'

'He's in Verona today and tomorrow, isn't he?'

'Yes, he has much to occupy him there,' he said, and she was surprised to hear the note of satisfaction in his voice.

They had reached the steps by the Danieli and, once more, Theresa felt like a caricature of a nurse following a surgeon, as they walked slowly into the hotel. Heads turned to watch them, even though the clothes worn by Venetians and tourists were varied and sometimes quite bizarre. They'll know me again, she thought, and I suppose will dismiss me as the nurse from the hotel. Dark eyes saw her and registered approval as the girl in plain white

with the flaming hair walked with head high beside
the handsome man who seemed oblivious of the
glances. 'You see, you need a uniform to protect
you,' he said.

The receptionist gave him the keys to the suite
and a pile of letters. Theresa waited helplessly,
while he riffled through the pile, took out one or
two and handed the others back saying, 'Signor
Ravenna.' He looked up, as if surprised that she
was still there. 'Well, aren't you going to get out of
those terrible clothes?'

'I haven't a key,' she said.

'I must change, too,' he said. 'Are you hungry?'

'I am, a little,' she said. 'Shall I have a meal in the
restaurant, or do you expect me to sit upstairs all
the evening?'

'Of course not. I'm taking you to dinner.' He
unlocked the door.' I have two calls to make but I
shall be ready in half an hour.' He grinned. 'Something cool enough to be comfortable but not so that
you inflame the natives.'

'But I thought you wouldn't be seen with me out
of uniform,' she said, weakly.

'My dear girl, I can't have dinner with a nurse.
All Venice would think I was an invalid,' he said,
with patient logic.

'Crazy,' she murmured as she put her uniform
with the rest of her soiled laundry. She was surprised to see the first white dress washed and
pressed and on a hanger again. I won't need that,
with any luck, she thought, but put it carefully in

the wardrobe as it was so beautifully pressed. She hummed a tune as she plucked two hairs from her eyebrows and added bronzy-gold eyeshadow. Almost defiantly, she selected a dress of thin cotton that swirled round her as she moved, the many colours mingling and separating and showing every curve of her body. It was cool and certainly not as extreme as some dresses she had seen, and her creamy skin and green eyes made her more striking than some of the suntanned beauties from the Lido. Bare legs with strappy sandals and pale nail varnish added to the freedom of her appearance and she wore a trace of pale lipstick.

Wasted on him, perhaps, but not quite what I'd wear if I went out with Luigi. She frowned. Pietro Bassano had made it quite clear that he was attracted to her when she arrived. Had that been pretence so that she would be afraid of all Italian men and so concentrate on her work and not get involved in a holiday affair? It must be that, she decided. He had shown no sign since of any emotion other than faint gratitude for her help at the operation in his clinic. It was his clinic, and so he needed to make it the best for his patients and for his own reputation as a surgeon. That was the only reputation he considered. To him, she was an attractive girl who might be a nuisance if she frittered away her time on pleasure when she could put her skills as a trained nurse to his benefit. She smiled, grimly. Well, tonight, Signor, we'll see if you are completely immune to me, even though I know Francesca has your attention and possibly your love, she thought. It would be interesting to notice any difference between his attitude towards her when they were alone, and tomorrow night when they would be with Francesca.

She heard movements in the sitting-room and opened her door. He was dressed in plain cream trousers with a dark red shirt of dull silk and she had to brace herself to appear casual, though her heart was thumping uncomfortably fast. His dark eyes flickered over her and he looked down at the room keys in his hand. 'Ready?' he said. 'I know a place where it will be cool and the food is good.'

'There was no need to give up your evening for me,' she said. He held the door open for her politely but didn't touch her as she passed by in the narrow space.

'We both must eat,' he said, 'And I have to feed you after all your hard work. 'Besides, there is something more I want from you, Theresa.'

As he called her by her name, a thrill of expectancy enveloped her and she turned to him in the corridor outside the suite, her lips slightly parted, her eyes shining. 'What is it?' she said.

'I have another case tomorrow and I would appreciate your help again,' he said.

CHAPTER FOUR

'I MAY go out alone?' Theresa looked across the breakfast table at the surgeon with puzzled eyes.

'You aren't a prisoner here,' Pietro Bassano replied. 'You are free to explore on your own with the help of a tourist map until lunch time, when you will return for a light lunch and then change into uniform again for the case this afternoon.'

'You don't think that I shall be abducted?' The sarcasm was evident. 'Is it safe between the hours of nine and twelve every morning?'

'Not every morning, but today Luigi will not be back here until we have left for dinner with Francesca and I think that you can manage any other importunate advances.' He smiled. 'Luigi must be very annoyed that he has to be away so much during the next week or so. Verona will take up a lot of time, then there is the visit to Rome, to Florence and back to Verona.' He smiled again with real humour. 'Poor Luigi!' He put down his coffee cup. 'You have enough money for shopping?'

'Of course. I have my salary and I'm not completely without means of my own,' she said, resenting the way that once more he made her feel as if he owned her but had no deep need of her. 'You said when I came that I should go home. I'm inclined to agree, now that I have had time to consider it. Left to myself here, I would be lonely and I am not doing the work for which I came. I love theatre work, but I could as easily have done that back at St Edmund's, among friends.'

His eyes held an expression that could have been anger or pain. 'Do you hate me so much, Theresa? Have I been too demanding? If so, I am sorry.'

She wanted to tell him that he had made none of the demands she wanted from him. She needed the demand of strong arms, a man's body taut against her own and kisses of passion and deep love. Last night she had dined with him, by a dark and glinting waterside, the cries of the gondoliers coming through the distant lamplight and the sky a deep velvet curtain. He had talked of Venice, of their work, and when they went back to the hotel, he had kissed her on the brow and thanked her for her company, leaving her to toss in her bed, wanting him as she had never thought it possible to want any man.

'I don't hate you, Pietro,' she said. 'If I'm to be back by twelve, I have a lot of sightseeing to do.' She rose from her seat at the breakfast table and turned away, wondering what his thoughts must be as she left. She went out into the bright sunshine and looked up at the cloudless sky. This could be paradise for two people in love, and less than nothing for a woman who could not arouse more than a passing desire in a good-looking man. She looked at the gondolas bobbing in the water at their striped mooring poles, and at the men who poled them, dressed in boldly striped blue and white tee-shirts and the debonair straw hats with colourful ribbons. She went along to San Marco, across which square she had walked last night with the tall, dark and very silent man who had only taken her to dinner to pay a debt.

The stones of the square were hot and the full light of morning was relentless on her bare head. She wandered along with a group of people who were on a package tour, led by a man holding aloft a huge umbrella to show his chicks which way he was going through the narrow streets. She let them go ahead and looked in shop windows at the wonderful and very expensive silk garments strewn with studied carelessness over slender chairs, Murano glass ornaments and wire cages. She bought a string of tiny glass elephants in pale pink. It would be something amusing to take back to England and might remind her of the lighter moments of her stay in Venice.

Masks of all colours and shapes were in the next window. There was a bright red devil mask made exactly as they were so long ago when masked balls were in fashion among the rich and famous in Italy, and she saw that these masks were copied from old paintings that hung in the back of the craftman's shop. She shuddered. What if she went to such a ball and found Luigi behind a devil's mask? But there was no need to think of him for a whole day.

The restrictions put on her by the work that

Pietro asked her to do and the constant supervision of her free time made her feel imprisoned, even if he denied that she was a prisoner. I'm mad to stay, she thought, but she knew that she couldn't leave yet, even if her heart was broken. I have to see him for just a little longer, she told herself. I have to hear his voice and his laugh even if his laughter isn't for me. She half dreaded the visit to the Cipriani to meet Francesca again. Could she bear to watch them—touching, bending over in a mutual exchange of thought, seeing their affection for each other?

She sat in a pavement café and watched the people and the boats on the canal by a tiny humped-back bridge and by the time she realised that it was late, she had explored only a tiny corner by the main square. She went back to the hotel and up to her room, using the key that she now had for her own use, to enter and leave the suite as she wished. Or as Pietro wishes, she reminded herself. The suite was empty, and she decided to shower before lunch, to slip into the same dress she had worn that morning and then to change quickly after lunch to go back to the clinic with the surgeon.

The water was soft and cool and she revelled in its freshness, patting her skin dry with fluffy towels and rubbing fragrant oil into her skin where the sun might make it sore. In a quarter of an hour she would be expected in the dining-room, but she had plenty of time. She sat wearing her bra and bikini pants while she filed down a snag on a toe-nail and smoothed the skin of her feet with cream. Her door was slightly open and she heard nobody at the outer door until a girl called. Theresa saw her put down a tray of glasses and small bottles. Unable to tell her that she had not ordered any drinks, Theresa tried to wave the tray away, but the girl shook her head and pointed to her watch, as if to say it had been ordered for this time.

As she turned to go back to her room, suddenly afraid that Pietro was coming to drink an aperitif with her before lunch, she heard the door again. 'Pietro?' she called, but there was no reply. She listened again then decided that the girl had not closed the door properly the first time and had now done so. It could only be the maid or Pietro, and after his chilly behaviour the night before, she had no fears that he would push his way into her bedroom. Her door opened wider and she turned to see Luigi standing there, his eyes devouring the picture before him of the girl with creamy skin and wonderful hair, in pale blue underwear that did nothing to hide her body. He advanced slowly, as if hypnotised, and she backed away. She ran for the door of her room when he was away from it and gained the sitting-room.

'I have thought of you all night and came back for a little time to see you. Come, *cara*, don't be afraid. I know that you like me or you would not have been so angry.'

She looked round, desperately. What did she have to *do* to convince him that she didn't want

him? Pietro had warned her that even anger made a —
man think that she was not indifferent to him and it
wasn't possible to ignore him now that he was
coming towards her with that look in his eyes, and
she was so vulnerable.

'I was going to have a drink,' she said in a shaky
voice, wondering if he had ordered it, but he
seemed surprised to find two glasses filled with ice
on the tray. He hesitated, now sharing her conviction that Pietro might be coming to the suite, and
she dashed back to her room, locking the door after
her. She heard the crash of glass as he tried to
follow, and the outer door slam. He's gone, she
thought with deep thankfulness and peeped out in
time to see Pietro standing there, his eyes dark with
anger and his fists clenched. Luigi backed away to
the hallway as Pietro called her name.

'I'm all right, I really am all right,' she said. He
relaxed, but a pulse beating in his throat told of
controlled rage.

'Get dressed,' he muttered. She slipped on her
dress again and came out into the sitting-room.

'Did he touch you?'

'No. I should have kept my door locked as you
said, but I thought that as he was away, there was
no danger,' she said in a low voice.

Luigi grinned feebly, and said something in Italian that made the surgeon's cheeks flush red. He
replied and Luigi left the suite, after grabbing a
briefcase that he had dropped in the hall.

Pietro seemed to shake his mind free of the

incident. He rang down to service and a maid came with a cloth to mop up the water from the spilled ice. She brought fresh glasses and more ice while he watched Theresa sitting by the window, nervously picking at her dress. He poured a little Campari from óne of the bottles on to the ice in each glass and topped it up with cold sparkling *acqua minerale* from the Dolomite mountains. He handed the first glass to her and she glanced up at him when she took it, noticing that he made every effort to avoid touching her fingers. He drank deeply. 'Good,' he said. 'Are you ready for lunch?'

'Thank you,' she said, in a low voice.

'For what? For rescuing you, for the drink, or should I thank you for convincing Luigi that I am less than a man and with me you feel safe?'

'But last night, you were . . .'

'The perfect English gentleman? I may be so in England, but here, I wouldn't like to bet on it, Nurse Callan. But don't be alarmed. I have no intention of proving my manhood to Luigi by raping you.'

When they reached the dining-room her cheeks were still flushed. She pecked at the delicious sea-food salad and refused wine. 'Very wise. We have work to do,' he said.

'You can do without me,' she burst out. 'I'm going home to people who like me and who understand me.'

'You are forgetting that you have accepted an invitation this evening.'

'I'm not needed there. You and Francesca are very close and there is no place for me with you there.'

'Francesca? Ah, yes. She is very dear to me.' His eyes seemed to probe her heart and she refused to look at him. 'You must come. She cannot forget your kindness and she hopes to see more of you.'

'I shall be gone soon. Unless she comes to England that isn't possible.'

'And when you leave Venice? Will you never return?'

'Venice is not for girls on their own. You were right. I should have taken the next plane back as soon as I knew that Sir Julian was dead.'

'Venice needs to be savoured slowly like a delicious food. It is necessary to look at it from every small *campo*, every canal, to tread each of the hundreds of bridges and to visit the wonders of her palaces.'

'But not alone,' she said in a low voice.

'Not alone,' he agreed. 'Could you bear to change now? Lock your door and I shall be waiting here in half an hour.'

He was back again to the professional man with no time to waste and she hurried to change, for once glad to put on the garments that set her apart from him as a woman. I might as well have worn uniform last night, she thought. He hardly looked at me all the evening. And as he saw her coming to the entrance of the hotel, he smiled, as if he preferred to see her as a nurse.

'What have you, today? You haven't briefed me yet and I can't even read the list in Italian.'

'Nothing as tiring as the last,' he said.

'Not a heart case?' He shook his head. 'A thoro-coplasty?' He flushed slightly. 'Just a routine case that anyone could take for you?'

'It could mean further surgery,' he said.

'But not today?'

'I have to see what is there first,' he said, almost defensively. 'I need you there in case we do decide to go on with something more.'

She regarded him with cold eyes. If he was only going to examine a patient using a bronchoscope to look into the lungs, he certainly didn't need a skilled nurse to help him. At St Edmund's, such investigations were done at the end of lists after the clean cases had gone back and it didn't matter too much if the theatre was made unclean. 'What do you suspect?' she said.

'Filipo works on a fruit barge and eats his way through much of his stock. He swallowed a peach stone and it went into his bronchus but didn't cut off his air passage. He coughed a little from time to time and I think brought up some stained sputum, but he had no idea that the fruit stone was still there. He has been ill at home and one day he collapsed. I think he has an abscess in his lung. With luck we may be able to take the foreign matter away through a bronchoscope and not do major surgery, but we must go carefully to avoid perfora-tion. The X-rays show patches that could be parts of the disintegrated peach husk, but we need to make a direct examination.' They arrived at the clinic. 'Come and see him before he comes to the theatre. He would like that.'

Theresa followed him to a cool room with long pale curtains floating at the windows giving an added illusion of calm freshness. A boy with huge dark eyes in a pale face stared at her and then smiled. She took his hand and it was slightly moist. The veins in his arms showed blue in the thin flesh and his breath was laboured. Pietro spoke to him and the boy smiled again. Theresa thought that Pietro was telling him that she was English and could speak no Italian, and it make her want to learn the language before she came back to Venice. If I come back, she remembered.

At the theatre Theresa was greeted as an old friend. The girl who liked to practise her English was there again, and this time Theresa knew where to change and where to scrub. She checked her trolley, knowing that this was a routine examination and as such was universal. She thought of the expression in the boy's eyes. She had asked Pietro what he had said. 'He said you were *simpatico*. You have the touch, and the skill for this place,' he said. 'He wants you to visit him after the operation. Even at seventeen, and ill, an Italian appreciates a pretty face.'

'I have to go back to do midwifery,' she said.

'Not for three months.'

'You have a good memory,' she said. 'But you

don't need me here. The nurses are well trained and could cope with anything you wanted done.'

'Every surgeon has his idiosyncrasies. Some like a special suture material, some like special swabs. I need you. I hope that something will make you change your mind and let you stay. You could work here and live here. You could have your own theatre with whatever staff you wanted.'

She tried to hide her surprise at the urgency in his voice. 'I have to go back. I could never get a place at the training school I want if I turned down this opportunity, and if I want my own theatre, I should know about such operations as Caesarian section. I am quite good at things other than thoracic theatre,' she said.

The door to the anaesthetic room opened and the boy was wheeled in on a trolley, looking half dead. A tray with a tracheotomy set was ready in case it was needed, but as yet the obstruction was too low for that to be of use. Only if he coughed and blocked the larynx completely would it be used. Theresa took one of the long, shining brass tubes that tapered slightly away from the eyepiece and was gently rounded to avoid hurting the delicate tissues of the throat and the lining of the bronchus. The boy's head rested on hard pillows to make a line from mouth to lungs through which the straight tube could pass and Pietro Bassano took it, lightly lubricated with water soluble jelly, and opened the mouth of the unconscious boy. Theresa stood ready with a sucker hissing in her hand, and a dish into which they hoped they might put any debris taken from the lung by means of long slender forceps. A light bulb at the far end of the tube was bright enough to illuminate the area being examined and Pietro bent to look through the tube.

Theresa picked up a square of polished glass from the trolley. 'You aren't wearing a shield on your headlamp,' she said, remembering the strict rule at St Edmund's that in all cases where a bronchoscope wàs used the surgeon should be protected by placing the glass between his eyes and the brass tube to that any discharge coughed out by the patient might be stopped from touching his face. Pietro stood back slightly and let her hold it in position. He took a pair of forceps and gently caught a grey bundle of exudate and brought it out on to the dish. In it were the remains of half a peach stone. He sucked out the crater made by the stone and went slightly deeper. The boy coughed slightly and they waited until he settled again. Theresa turned to put the specimen in a tube for the pathological department, wondering, after all this time, and noting the boy's general appearance, if tuberculosis might have added to his illness. She signed to the nurse to seal the tube and the girl who spoke English made sure that the order was carried out. Another piece of material came from the next probing, this was some more stone, fragmented and impossible to see if the fragments made up a complete half. Once more, they cleared the area with suction and Pietro was almost satisfied that he had drained away all discharge. He asked the anaesthetist to let the boy come back a little so that his cough reflex came into being. The boy coughed and then settled again and the sleep deepened once more. The next probe brought up a little more and Pietro said that even if there was a little left, antibiotics and breathing exercises and perhaps one more bronchoscopy would be all that was needed.

He took one final look but waved aside the square of glass that Theresa held to protect his eyes, muttering that it was cloudy. In a lighter sleep, the boy coughed violently sending a shower of exudate over the face of the surgeon.

'Saline and swabs and bowls!' called Theresa, hoping they understood. She dragged Pietro to a chair, motioning to the other doctor to take out the bronchoscope and finish the case. As the nurse brought the bowl of warm saline, Theresa stood behind the surgeon and sent a constant trickle of water from the inner corner of one eye to drain outwards and then the same on the other eye, letting most of it fall into dishes held by other nurses, but not really caring where it went as long as it was carried away from his eyes. She swabbed his face and repeated the treatment until she was completely satisfied that his eyes and face were clear. She took a towel and dried his face, using clean swabs to dry each eye and called for eyedrops.

'What do they have here? Sulphacetamide?' she asked, hoping that the name was international. The nurse nodded and brought a phial with a clean dropper. Theresa checked to see that it was the correct solution and saw that it was the strong dosage, 30% solution. She instilled drops into each eye and waited while he blinked away the excess. Only then did she realise that his head was gently pillowed on her now rather damp breast. She raised his head and he shook his head. 'Are you all right?' she asked.

'Now that you've finished drowning me,' he said, mildly. 'But thank you. I was a fool to take that risk.' It was his first admission to any weakness and her heart warmed to him. At last he seemed human.

'The drops were stronger than you should have as a follow up,' she said. 'Can you ask if they have any 10% to take with you?'

'I can't put in drops,' he said, with a slow smile. 'I shall have to have a nurse.'

She blushed, knowing that the drops should be instilled as frequently as every four hours to make an umbrella of safety after such an accident. 'You could stay here, where you have rooms,' she said, sweetly. 'I'm sure that there would be round-the-clock volunteers.'

'I have to take a lady to dinner tonight,' he said. 'So you, my dear Nurse Callan, must come too.'

'Does that mean I have to go to the Cipriani in uniform?'

He had the grace to look embarrassed. 'No, you wear your prettiest dress tonight because there will be many lovely women there.'

'Do your eyes feel soothed? I wonder if I should put more drops in before you go back to the hotel?'

'I have a patient to see first, but perhaps you should examine them again before we leave.' To her, the glint in his eyes was not just from the drops—unless Sulphacetamide made a man look wicked. She smiled, secretly, and nodded as if agreeing. He went to the ward where the patient from the previous day was recovering well and Theresa changed into her uniform dress ready to leave. When Pietro came back, she showed him to a surgical chair rather like one used by dentists, and he had to sit on it while she shone a light and put in more drops from a safe distance, so he couldn't cradle his head on her bosom. It was satisfying to note that he found the chair uncomfortable and stayed in it for the minimum time, flicking away the drops almost as soon as she instilled them into his eyes.

Theresa packed the eye drops and swabs in her holdall and asked if she could borrow some small absorbent towels which she could use to pad the space between the dish catching excess fluid and the neck of the patient. If Pietro Bassano was dressed in a silk shirt, he would not want trickles of eye-drops to be spilled over it when it was time for the treatment at the Cipriani. He eyed her preparations with amusement mixed with respect.

'If it was another surgeon, you would insist on these simple precautions,' she said. 'I've noticed that every man working in hospital believes that he is immune from injury or infection by some divine right, but bullies every other person who is exposed to risk.'

'It's true,' he admitted. 'But aren't you being rather fussy taking all those things to the hotel?'

'It's partly cowardice,' she said. 'If you needed something that I didn't have in this bag, I would have no idea what to ask for in a chemist's shop. I don't even know what shop I would look for unless it had soap and beauty preparations in the window as they do at home.'

'And you like to be prepared for every emergency. I like that.' She sensed that he wanted to thank her far more than he had done, but found it difficult. By praising her attitude to work, it became less personal but still showed that he noticed her efficiency. 'I asked you to think about taking a job here for the time left before you go back to another training. Think carefully before you refuse. I need you here to help me train new staff and I also need you because I have to concentrate on my surgery and not on what is happening in the theatre.'

She blushed. It was the longest speech of praise she had heard from him and she was touched, even though she would have given all that praise for a tender glance that spoke of a deeper need, for a woman with soft and willing arms and a warm heart. 'Have you finished here, or do you want to visit the wards?' she said.

'We'll go now. A rest before we change might be a good idea. We can have tea on the balcony if that

would please you.' He must have been more upset
by the infected material going into his eyes than he
admitted, she thought. His manner was friendly
and attentive and she prayed that it might be so for
a long time.

'Tea, more drops and change. Is that the programme?' she said.

'If you insist.' But he smiled and she knew that he
was grateful for her care.

The light on the water seemed to have an added
silver radiance as the water taxi skimmed back to
the Danieli. The two passengers were relaxed and
Theresa couldn't keep her mouth from smiling. To
work in Venice with this man would be wonderful
from a professional point of view, and the fact that
he had asked her made her heart sing with pleasure
and triumph, but, as a woman, she knew that it
would be impossible. Here on the water, with the
life of the city about them, it was easy to be
lighthearted, to be told about the local sights and
the history of many of the ancient buildings, but if
she stayed, there would be times when they would
be thrown together alone, perhaps when tired, or
very elated because a case that had given anxiety
was going right, and they would have that bond of
shared achievement that is so precious in their
professions. Could she hide her growing love for
him if this happened? At St Edmund's, after night
emergencies, she had often been hugged and even
kissed after a case, meaning 'thank you and aren't

we a clever team?' and nothing more than that certain bond. It would be impossible to accept such affectionate, casual overtures from Pietro Bassano. If he put his arms round my shoulders, in weariness or because everything had gone well, I would sink into his arms, return his light kiss with passion and disgrace myself by showing how much I wanted him, she thought.

'You are sad. Were you thinking about the boy we left just now?'

'Yes,' she lied. 'Do you think he will be all right?' She glanced at him, trying to see if his eyes looked sore. 'When do you have the result of the path. tests?'

'You are afraid he has TB too, aren't you?'

She stared. It was something she had pushed to the back of her mind. If the boy had tuberculosis, the risk to the dark eyes that now stared back at her was increased. 'It did cross my mind,' she said. 'If the tests are positive, you will have to have a smear taken, won't you?' She made her voice noncommittal, as if it were a routine safeguard.

'You will do it for me?'

'You mean, today?' A cold feeling engulfed her under the hot charged air.

'I brought a loop and a couple of tubes,' he said. 'I didn't want to panic them back there, but I think it might be wise.' He smiled, seeing her sudden anxiety. 'Not that a single bacillus could possibly remain after your onslaught. My main worry was drowning,' he said, and his smile was warm and caring, almost like the smile he gave to Francesca when he bent over her at the funeral luncheon.

'That means a slight risk,' she said. 'As I recall from the eye ward, you can't get a genuine reading from eyes already covered with antibiotic drops. Don't you think you should wait until you know the results of the boy's tests? If he has TB and you stop your treatment, you might miss the chance of a quick all-clear.' She wondered if she was taking too much responsibility for him and if she might anger him by putting her views strongly but she knew what must be said. 'I'd be more inclined to continue the drops until you have built a barrier to kill whatever infection is there. If the tests come back positive, all the more reason for you to have intensive treatment at the beginning. Would you have to change the drops if the tests showed TB?

'Probably not. We were fortunate to have the right ones ready, but I might have to have a course of anti-TB drugs such as streptomycin if my swab was positive, but that would be decided by an eye man.' She sighed with relief. 'Don't worry. I'm too concerned with my own health to take risks. So far, I have been very fortunate. I am sound in mind and limb, as the British say, my eyes are good and my heart as strong as one of the lions on the basilica.'

'I would never have guessed,' she said, with a smile.

'And you, Nurse Callan? Is your heart strong and true and beating for someone with a steady pulse of love?'

'It fibrillates sometimes,' she said, and hoped that he couldn't know how fast her pulse was at that moment.

'I know so little about you. I know that you are an excellent nurse who is respected and liked by all the staff who have met you.' She inclined her head with a smile that made her eyes bright sparks of green light. 'You have no opinion of Italian men and you give off an air of untouchable virginity that is quite rare and, to someone like Luigi, quite irresistible.' She blushed. 'But you are safe now that he is back among his papers and lawyers.'

'That's a relief,' she said, longing to ask if he found that look of untouchable virginity attractive, or off-putting.

'The Danieli and tea,' he said, jumping ashore and taking the cases from the boatman. He hurried ahead, leaving her to bring her smaller bag and to find a way between the gathered tourists assembling obediently with their guide before looking at the Doge's palace. She wondered at his many moods and decided that if she was an unknown quantity to him, then he was far more of an enigma. In the boat, she had once more felt that charge of magnetism between them, but now she was just a nurse, carrying his eyedrops up to the suite they shared so impersonally.

It was easy to gaze into a man's eyes when standing at his back and looking at him upside-down. Theresa smiled. Eyes from this position were the eyes of a patient and no particular one. Meekly, he settled back in the chair with his head resting on the cushion that padded the top of the back, and stared up at the ceiling. 'No irrigation?' he said.

'Not this time, or when you are at the Cipriani. We'll give the drops time to build up their potency and I'll irrigate before you go to bed tonight. I borrowed an Undine irrigator and they boiled it for me and put it in a sterile bag. I have enough lotion to last until you go back to the clinic and you have the weaker drops to be used tomorrow.'

He looked up, the healthy white of his eyes tiny-veined, with a faint almost babyish blue in the sclera, and the long dark lashes curling and moist. Theresa instilled the drops and he blinked. She wiped away any that remained on his cheek and repeated the process on the other side. A lock of dark hair hung over her hand as she put in the last drop and the moisture ran down his cheek. 'I thought you had a rock-steady hand, Nurse Callan.'

'We all have our weak moments,' she murmured.

'And what of tonight?' He was laughing at her. 'I saw on the bottle that the drops have to be given every four hours. Shall I wake you, or will you wake me when they are due?'

'That isn't necessary,' she said, shortly. 'I'm using the full strength at midnight so that the next dose can be omitted, then we start on the weaker ones before breakfast.'

'You have everything worked out, Nurse Callan.

Is your whole life planned like your work in the theatre? What will you do when you tire of wearing a mask and handing instruments?'

'I'm doing midwifery,' she said.

'Ah, yes, I was forgetting.' A girl arrived with a vast tray of tea and cream cakes and put it on the table on the shady balcony. Theresa poured tea, feeling slightly odd as she still wore uniform. 'You even pour tea efficiently,' he said, as if it was a sin.

'It's the uniform you insisted that I wore,' she said.

'I suppose so. It helps to make you look very businesslike, and very much the career woman.'

'And the Italian part of you dislikes women's lib? Do you secretly believe that a woman should stay at home?'

'Some women, who want to do so. Others who would not be a success at home-making are welcome to work as men.'

'That's not fair. A woman needn't lose her femininity because she works, but people like Francesca have no need to work and so you think that they are the only ones who are feminine.'

'Francesca works,' he said. She looked up in surprise and saw that he was annoyed. 'Francesca runs a very successful fashion house with branches in Florence and London.' He put down his empty cup and brushed the crumbs from his lap. 'Francesca was widowed two years ago and has worked hard ever since. She is one of the few women I know who could do as she does and stay as appealing.'

'I didn't know,' said Theresa. 'Has she any children?'

'No. There wasn't time.' He stared out at the busy scene below. 'And she is one who should have children.'

'She is very lovely,' said Theresa.

'And when her period of mourning is over, she will marry again,' he said, with a tender smile. 'Dear Francesca, who has waited so patiently for so long.'

'I think I should be getting ready,' said Theresa. Her heart ached. He was waiting for the period of mourning to be over before he could marry his heart's love, and he could praise Francesca's patience with no hint of his own long frustration. When he had warned Theresa to lock her door even against himself, he was longing for Francesca and needed an outlet, any outlet for his desire, and feared that he might be indiscreet. Well, he seems to be firmly under control now, she thought bitterly. He will be seeing his darling girl this evening, so I expect I could wander about stark naked and he wouldn't notice me tonight.

CHAPTER FIVE

'AND you really do not mind that there will be others here having dinner with us?'

'Of course not, Francesca,' Theresa said. 'I shall be happy with any arrangement that you like to make. It's good of you to invite me at all, but if there are people coming who need to talk to you about private matters, please say and I will stay here.'

'No, it is you and Pietro I want to have as my guests and perhaps one or two others, but when Sir Julian's friends wanted to see me again before they left, I had to invite them, too. At least there will be someone who speaks English and who can talk freely to you. One of the Americans who made up his team is coming and would like to meet you.'

'Is it to be a big party?' Theresa was uneasy. 'What are you wearing?'

'It will be ten for dinner and some more are joining us for coffee later. As to clothes, you will look charming whatever you wear, Theresa. With that wonderful hair, who will notice what you wear?'

'You mean that everyone will be very smartly dressed,' said Theresa, sensing that Francesca took it for granted that her clothes could never come up to the standard of the wealthy people with whom she associated. 'I'll have to look out a simple little number I brought with me,' she said, as if she would treat it as a joke.

'Is Pietro there?' Francesca wanted to know. She had been talking to Theresa on the telephone for five minutes and as yet he hadn't returned to the suite from the desk.

'I could ring down and see if he is there,' said Theresa, 'But he should be back now. He said he was going to fetch the mail and to enquire about boats.'

The outer door opened. Pietro strode into the sitting-room and Theresa beckoned him to the telephone, saying that it was Francesca on the line.

'Francesca! *Cara.*' There followed a string of fast Italian from Francesca and Pietro responded in the same language. Theresa slipped away, overhearing her name but having no idea what was being said about her. As always, she hated to hear them talking as if she wasn't there and she wondered why she was mentioned at all.

Whatever was said, it was soon over and she heard Pietro humming to himself as he went into the bathroom. Theresa was glad that she had already washed her hair and put on a dress while it dried and so was fairly respectable when called to the telephone in the open sitting-room. I'm learning fast, she thought. She rubbed her hair vigorously and brushed it into shape, letting it dry naturally in the warm air. She found her bronzy-pink eye

make-up and painted her finger and toenails a
coppery pink that toned with the bronze and gold
straps of her slender-heeled sandals. It's much too
hot for tights, she decided. Italian women might be
able to look cool in long sleeves and tights, but I
must feel fairly comfortable.

Her first instinct was to choose something fairly
plain to wear that would fit into most situations but
draw little attention to herself. But every time
Francesca mentioned clothes, possibly because she
knew so much about them through her boutiques
and her international contacts, her tone had been
faintly disparaging, even if she meant nothing in-
sulting.

Theresa tightened her lips. Pietro didn't want her
as a woman, Francesca thought she was something
completely outside the fashion scene and she
couldn't make friends with Italian men like Luigi or
they would think she was ready to jump into bed
with them. 'Life is hard for a working girl,' she told
her reflection. She laughed. Why not give it everything? Let Pietro see her flirting with the American, perhaps, or at least let him know that she
didn't have to do everything he told her. More and
more, she had the impression that he was watching
her, making sure she did nothing out of line and
came to no harm. It was good up to a point, but was
becoming quite claustrophobic. He doesn't want
me, but he'd like to make quite sure that I remain
the nice little nurse ready to work for him, expecting nothing in the way of a human relationship from

him. What did it matter to him what she said, when he was in love with Francesca and planning marriage and a family with her as soon as she felt that the time was right to forget her first marriage and to take a new husband?

The finely-pleated sheath flowed over her arm as she took it from its enclosing cylinder which protected the pleats, making them stay firm and clinging and yet so supple that when she let the dress fall to one side, it fanned out like a butterfly wing, delicate and beautiful. She put it on over her flesh-coloured bra and pants and wore only a thick gold chain round her throat, a present from her grandmother, who in turn had received it from her mother. Tiny jade earrings, hidden but glimpsed briefly under her hair, finished the effect she wanted and the new fan of Venetian lace in dull bronze would be useful both to cool her face and to have in her hand as something to give confidence if she was uneasy.

Pietro tapped on the door. 'Five minutes?' he said. 'I have a boat coming to pick us up.'

'I thought we were going in the Cipriani launch,' she replied through the door.

'There are several others going in that. I made my own arrangements.' So he was keeping her aloof from the other guests until he could hand her over to Francesca and the American who would tag on to her and be her bodyguard all the evening. 'Bring a coat or something,' he said. 'It may be cool when we come back tonight.'

Theresa picked up the gossamer shawl that she had been unable to resist at a London sale. The assistant had fingered it with envy, wrapped it and said, 'I've wanted it ever since it came in to dress the window, but when would I wear it?' In Venice, now, seemed the answer, and she stepped out of her room and closed the door behind her.

Pietro was wearing a suit of pale silk with a crimson cummerbund and a matching shirt. His hair was freshly washed and curling and the dark eyes were like live coals of light as he saw the girl come from her room. He stared for a moment.

'Will I do?' she said.

'It depends,' he said, cryptically. 'Can you put in cuff-links?' He held out his hands and she saw that he held something of gold with the sparkle of rubies in his hand. 'I always forget until I'm dressed, and then it's awkward,' he said. She took one link and pushed it through the buttonhole, bringing the cuff up to meet it. She could feel his eyes taking in every detail of her bare shoulders and her hair, and she kept her head low. The second cuff had tighter buttonholes and she had to work at it for a moment. Then it was done and she made as if to stand straight. A tremor of delirious pleasure filled her as his lips brushed the bare neck where her hair parted as she bent down. 'Thank you,' he said, in a low voice, and her heart told her that, even if he loved Francesca, he wanted *her* for that moment. She drew away as if she had noticed nothing and folded her shawl.

'Your eyes seem fine,' she said.

'I didn't think you had looked at them.'

'A good nurse observes without seeming to do so,' she said, demurely. 'I hope that out of uniform I won't be an embarrassment to you.'

'Where did you get that dress?'

'A little thing I picked up in case I had to have dinner with Sir Julian,' she said. 'It will come in useful when I get back. Mr Nuttall gives a big party each year and I am invited before going to Charlotte's.'

'I shall look at you and say, "That old thing again!"—I have been invited, too.'

'You'll have to pretend that it's new,' she said.

'No, I shall be glad to see it because it means that we meet again, even if it is not your wish.' He looked at her sadly.

'I am here,' she said, and shrugged.

'And this evening, we must have a good time because Francesca is better, my eyes are all right, thanks to you, and I assure you that the company and food will be excellent.' He seemed to be making a determined effort to speak naturally, but, once more, Theresa noticed a pulse throbbing in his cheek. He was more worried about his eyes than he admitted, she thought. She was almost certain that he would have no lasting ill effects from the accident in the theatre, and he obviously was very relieved and grateful. Well, I'm all dressed up and if I have to make do with gratitude, and acceptance that I am efficient, that will have to do.

'I intend to have a very good time,' she said.

The receptionist glanced at them as they passed and then looked again. The same thing happened as they left the foyer and other guests were going into the restaurant. Theresa stole a glance at the proud face and wondered if he was regretting her appearance as she left the hotel with him. Nobody could say she looked like a nurse now. How would he explain to himself or to any other interested person the transformation from nurse to . . . what?

Italian men turned to stare with no attempt to hide their interest and envy, but Pietro marched on and she followed, trying to walk well in her high heels. 'Are we catching a bus?' she gasped. He slackened his steps. 'I could have put a sack over my head if you didn't want to be seen with me,' she said. 'But I can't walk any faster in these shoes.'

The steps led down to a gondola and Pietro went first and put out a hand for her. He was silhouetted against the dark boat with the velvet cushions, the sparkling evening light on the water and the gondolier with the traditional carved wooden rest for the oar. She caught her breath. It was as if she had glimpsed his ancestor being taken in the gondola with the livery of the family, even though this was today and the gondolier was wearing man-made fibres in his shirt and the well-cut silk suit of her escort was of the latest Italian design.

She stepped into the well of the boat and the evening breeze lifted folds of her dress, thrusting it against her thighs and billowing it out behind her.

Love, romance, intrigue...all are captured
for you by Mills & Boon's top-selling authors.

TAKE FOUR
EXCITING BOOKS
ABSOLUTELY FREE

Four exciting Mills & Boon
Romances have been specially selected
for you to enjoy FREE and without
any obligation. You'll fall in love with
the fascinating characters, the
intrigue and the exotic locations of
these marvellous stories. Each
romance will hold you spellbound
from the first page to the last
loving embrace. To find out how
you can claim your FOUR FREE
BOOKS, please turn over.

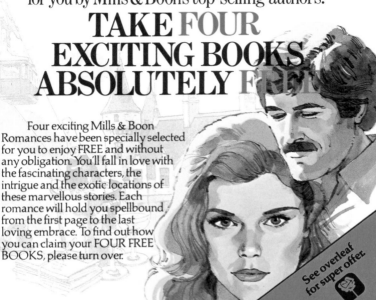

See overleaf
for super offer.

Mills & Boon, the world's most popular publisher of romantic fiction, invites you to take these four books free.

FOUR BOOKS FREE

As a special introductory offer to the Mills & Boon Reader Service, we will send you four superb Mills & Boon Romances ABSOLUTELY FREE and WITHOUT OBLIGATION. Become a subscriber, and you will receive each month:

 THE NEWEST ROMANCES – reserved at the printers and delivered direct to you by Mills & Boon.

 POSTAGE AND PACKING FREE – you only pay the same as you would in the shops.

 NO COMMITMENT – you receive books only for as long as you want.

 FREE MONTHLY NEWSLETTER – keeps you up-to-date with new books and book bargains.

 HELPFUL, FRIENDLY SERVICE from the girls at Mills & Boon. You can ring us any time on 01-684 2141.

THE FOUR FREE BOOKS SHOWN HERE ARE OUR SPECIAL GIFT TO YOU. THEY ARE YOURS TO KEEP REGARDLESS OF WHETHER YOU WISH TO BUY FURTHER BOOKS.

Just fill in and post the coupon today.

Mills & Boon

Mills & Boon Reader Service,
PO Box 236, Croydon,
Surrey CR9 3RU.

NO STAMP NEEDED

FREE BOOKS CERTIFICATE

To: Mills & Boon Reader Service, PO Box 236, Croydon, Surrey CR9 9EL.

Please send me, free and without obligation the four Mills & Boon Romances illustrated in this leaflet, and reserve a Reader Service Subscription for me. If I decide to subscribe I shall, from the beginning of the month following my free parcel of books, receive six new books each month for £5.70 post and packing free. If I decide not to subscribe, I shall write to you within 14 days. The free books are mine to keep in any case.
I understand that I may cancel my subscription at any time simply by writing to you. I am over 18 years of age.

Please write in BLOCK CAPITALS

Name_____

Address_____

_____

_____ Post Code_____

 SEND NO MONEY – TAKE NO RISKS.   10D 36

One offer per household. Offer applies in UK only – overseas send for details. If price changes are necessary you will be notified.

She sat down, but not before a passing man called 'Bellissima' and paused to watch them depart. Pietro was beside her, looking at the far shore of Giudecca where the Cipriani Hotel was situated. Passing *vaporetti* made small waves but the gondola was stable and moved fast across the water. She glanced back at the Doge's palace, golden in the last rays of the sun, and sighed. 'I haven't really seen Venice,' she said, 'and I must go soon.'

'You have decided to leave? You refuse to come to the clinic?'

'I can't.' She saw his mouth tighten, and wished she had said nothing tonight. If his plans for a well-run theatre were dashed, he might well be bad-tempered and spoil the evening. 'It's all too difficult,' she said. 'I feel at a disadvantage, knowing so little Italian, something might happen that I couldn't manage.'

'You coped with one sudden emergency very well and there would be someone at each case who spoke English, apart from me.'

'Let's forget it for today. So much has happened that I am confused,' she begged, her eyes wide and her trembling lips vulnerable. How could he know that the difficulties were not of language, but because she couldn't bear to be near to him in a working situation, knowing that the relationship ended there at the door of the operating theatre? She hated herself for loving him, knowing him to be all the things she most wanted to avoid in the man she loved. He was arrogant, unfeeling and would work her to death and see no reason why he should not do so, turning to Francesca for love and relaxation and the filling of his leisure hours. While I scrub instruments, he could be on his way over the water, to his love and his future.

'We'll talk about it again later,' he said. 'There is a lot that we have to discuss, Theresa.'

'Later,' she said. 'Now, tell me what this island is about.'

'That is San Georgio Maggiore. One day, you must climb the tower or *campanile* and look back at San Marco. It gives the best view of Venice. It is still a monastery and you may find a young monk working the lift when you go there. The canal here is the canal of Giudecca by the next string of small islands. I think you'll like it there.' He was talking as if he were reading a guide book and not taking in anything he read. It did nothing to dispel the growing tension that she felt as his shoulder pressed against her, his thigh against her leg where they sat together looking ahead, with the rhythmic strokes of the oar sending them further across the canal. His hand touched hers as it lay in the soft fabric of her dress. She tried to ignore it, but his fingers curled round her own, as if taking a small bird in his grasp, delicately so as not to hurt it. He spread her fingers and looked at the nail varnish. 'How clever of you to get everything just right,' he said. She should have been pleased at the slightly oblique compliment, but she knew that he only admired her efficiency once more. Trust Nurse Callan to match everything, to have it all . . . just right. I wish I'd worn a . . . a red rose or something to clash badly with my scheme, she thought. At least it would prove that I was human and not too calculating.

The gondola turned in an arc to tie up at the poles by the jetty as the soft night was misting over the colours of day. Pietro said something to the gondolier and laughed. The man laughed, too, and turned to a couple who wanted to cross the canal with him. Once more, Theresa wondered if the men were talking and laughing about her. They stood for a few moments watching the gondola against the rosy light. Pietro put a hand under her elbow with more care than he had shown when they left the hotel and they walked between arches of wisteria, in a green gloom of false dusk.

'This is cool,' she said.

He stopped and looked at her. 'You look as cool as a lemon ice,' he said. 'And as delectable.' She fluttered her eyelashes over the green eyes that wanted to tell him so much. 'The sirocco is going and tomorrow will be much cooler.'

'Better for walking, better for tempers, perhaps,' she said.

'It's true that the sirocco hits men with a fury that upsets them. That is why you must be careful. Men like cool things when the heat hits them.'

She tried to turn away to look at the fast disappearing gondola that had borne them over the water of the Giudecca canal with flowing ease, but his hands were on her shoulders.

'It's easy for men to make the sirocco their excuse for their weakness,' she said.

He crushed her in his arms, his mouth an urgent, passionate statement of desire. 'Is this weakness? Or this? Or this?' His eyes glared darkly as he kissed her with a fury of anger and hurt pride. 'Have you no idea what effect you have on men used only to the dark beauty of their own women?'

She arched her back to push him away but his body came closer and her head turned, helplessly as an exotic orchid on a slender stalk, tied to a stronger, firmer stake that would not let the breeze take it. His need for her body was frightening and she tore his arms from her, and, shuddering at her own reactions, sank on to a stone seat under a rose bush. He was at her side, his hands trembling but no longer demanding. He put a hand under her chin and gazed into her bright eyes.

'You sneer at Luigi for having no control or respect for women. How can you justify this?' she said. She was shaking. If only he loved her as she wanted to be loved. If only he was not just attracted by green eyes and auburn hair and the fact that her dress revealed every line of her body, she would gladly sink into his embrace and tell him that she loved him and wanted him and would resist no longer.

His mouth was bitter. 'Can you be so innocent? I can't believe that you have never experienced love.'

'I don't call that love,' she said, recovering her

spirit. Was he saying that she must have slept around and so had to be kept from men in Venice while she was helping him with his work, just to preserve his reputation? 'You needn't worry,' she said, scornfully. 'I haven't found Italian men so fascinating that I want to make a fool of myself over them.'

'No?' His smile appeared, reluctantly and soft. 'I had another impression just now, but I suppose that it only showed that you are human, with all the expected biological responses.'

'I hate you,' she said. 'You humiliate me at every opportunity. I shall go home and forget everything that has happened here.'

He kissed her again, gently, and she trembled. Oh God, she prayed, I can't bear it much longer. Let him be rough and blatantly demanding, but not this hint of tenderness.

'You see, I am very controlled. You have seen nothing, Theresa. If I lost control, as you think I did just now, you would have no chance of escape.' He touched the line of one eyebrow and his finger traced the line of her cheekbone to the corner of her mouth. 'If I really lost control you could lock your door, your heart and your soul and I would find you! Climb to the top of the *campanile* in San Marco and hide behind the Greek horses! If I wanted you for my own, you would know the sirocco, believe me.'

She sat as if turned to stone. He knew that she responded to his passion and he was mocking her.

He loved Francesca and was only showing his power over other women, even if they said they were unwilling. 'I shall go home tomorrow,' she said. 'I shall go back to a place where men respect me, and get on with my life in peace.'

She had to allow him to hold her arm as she stumbled over the warm red bricks lining the walk. He looked down at her. 'Cheer up. You wouldn't like it if men didn't want you, and I assure you that, this evening, you could make any man crazy for you.'

'I think you should wipe away that lipstick,' she said, sweetly. 'Or they will all be quite convinced that you've brought your English mistress to dinner.' She handed him a clean tissue. 'You see, under this dress is the nurse who is prepared for all eventualities, just as you want her. A kind of machine. Please don't make the mistake of expecting human responses, Signor. That programme is not for you on my little built-in computer. Let's keep it separate, and I hope that I find someone more amusing to talk to this evening.'

'Theresa! Come back here.'

But she walked quickly towards the bright lights of the hotel and waved to Francesca who was looking out for them.

'You look wonderful,' said Francesca. 'That dress is perfect.' Her genuine admiration did much to soothe the girl's troubled spirit.

'I must get tidy. There was quite . . . a breeze and my hair is mussed-up.'

'Under no circumstances will you touch it. Each time I have met you, it has been so much under control that I wanted to get my hairdresser to do it for you in the style that suggests that the Signorina has been—how is the terrible expression?—tumbling in the hay?' She laughed. 'You have achieved something of that look. Not too much, but enough to show the woman and not the fashion model.'

'Is that how I look?' Francesca stared as the girl with the lovely hair giggled. 'I must be careful not to look too abandoned. It's wonderful to see you, and, as usual, you look superb.'

Francesca smiled. 'It is good when women can praise each other and mean it. I brought this dress from my shop in Florence. Come and sit with me before the others arrive. I asked you to come early as I must get to know you better.'

Theresa was touched by her manner and felt slightly guilty for thinking that the invitation was just a polite thank-you for services rendered. A waiter brought slim flutes of Murano glass filled with cold champagne.

'Pietro has disappeared, but it isn't important. I want to have you to myself.' Francesca smoothed the soft chiffon stole away from her delicate shoulders and revealed the low neckline of the pale pink silk dress. A necklace of deep coral set in gold was matched by heavy coral earrings and Theresa was amused and rather pleased to see that she carried a fan, too, though Francesca's was no souvenir lace fan, but a soft confection of silk and black feathers against a filigree of pure gold.

Her gaze wandered towards the water as she talked and Theresa wondered if she expected Pietro to come into the room from that direction. What could she do against a woman who had everything? The evident wealth showed in the ease with which Francesca expected good service in one of the most expensive hotels on the lagoon and in the quality of her shoes and handbag. Her beauty had dignity and culture and any man would worship her if she raised one pink-tipped finger. She told Theresa about her marriage almost as if it was a cautionary tale to be taken as a personal warning.

'I can speak of it now without emotion,' she said. 'For a long while I was harassed with guilt because I could not weep for him.' Theresa looked shocked. 'No, I think I know what is in your mind. I was not so upset that I was dry-eyed with no feelings. I didn't miss him. I thought, as a wife I must have some sorrow, but it wasn't so. I liked him for a time, as a friend, but marriage killed even that.'

'Why did you marry him?' Theresa stared at the lovely woman. 'You could have had any man you wanted.'

'It was a marriage between two old families and I was too well brought up to refuse when my father told me of his choice. It all seemed rather romantic and I had not then fallen in love.' Her eyes wandered again to look at the darkening water.

'And you met someone after you married?'

'Yes. I fell in love and had to send him away. But now, my official period of mourning has been over for some time. I owed that much to my family. I console myself that I have observed all the conventions.'

Theresa saw again how important were the outward signs of conventional behaviour among the cultured families of Venice. Who would care if Francesca married again within six months of her husband's death anywhere but in this strangely medieval city? And what a strain it must put on the desires of a man like Pietro who had to hide his feelings, until such a time as it was considered suitable for the declaration of their love. It was easy to understand his frustration and the difficulty he had to behave correctly with someone like Theresa, who was thrown in his path and forced to be close to him, physically, during the work they did together.

'I had no idea,' said Theresa.

'You have never been in love?' Francesca sighed. 'It is heaven and the other place all at the same time. I can't believe that I can now choose to live as I want, with the man I love.' She regarded Theresa solemnly. 'I think you know exactly what I mean. Is it bad that you are separated from your loved one?'

'He doesn't know that I love him,' said Theresa simply.

'He doesn't? Then you must make sure he knows.' She laughed. 'I cannot believe that he is indifferent to someone as attractive as you are.'

Theresa shook her head. 'I want to enjoy meeting new people and talking to you. Let's not talk about that.' How could she tell Francesca that she was in love with Pietro? Even worse, she could never say that he was the type of man to try to make love to a girl, when he was on his way to see the woman he loved.

Francesca tapped her knee with the fan and smiled. 'I want you to meet some very dear friends and some members of the Venice Restoration Fund. I met them some time ago when I became interested in helping to raise funds and we have gone a long way since then.' She went slightly pink and one hand fingered the coral at her throat. 'Here they are,' she said.

Pietro Bassano had two men with him. They came across the room to Francesca and stood by the low settle on which she was arranged so gracefully, with her now nearly recovered sprained ankle hidden under the folds of the billowy dress and the other slim foot peeping out on the velvet of the upholstery.

'May we join you?' Theresa looked up, surprised. The face was Italian, the voice American. He looked at Theresa with a wide smile. 'And I know all about you,' he said. 'George Clemente, and this is Hugo Maltby, my friend and colleague.' Theresa found her hand engulfed in the huge mitt of the second of the Americans who beamed at her with admiration and complete lack of inhibition.

'Great meeting you, Theresa. You look good enough to eat.'

Why was it that she could smile with pleasure at his words and the accompanying squeeze he gave to her hand, but would have stiffened if Pietro had done that. Hugo was so transparently honest and without any of the deviousness she had come to suspect in most of the men she met, that it was like a gust of fresh air. She laughed. 'I hope I'm not on the menu,' she said.

Francesca looked at Pietro enquiringly. He nodded and she slid from her perch and stood with the help of George who seemed to have taken complete charge of her. 'Dinner is ready and I am starving,' said Francesca. 'Come! Hugo will take Theresa and I shall have two stalwart men to help me.'

The rest of the party were waiting for them at the entrance to the restaurant and in a few minutes they were seated by the wide windows, open to the warm night. Lights were coming on all over Venice and flickered like tiny candles over the calm water of the lagoon. It was a perfect setting of luxury and beauty, with elegant women and handsome well-dressed men, and quiet, efficient service.

Theresa glanced round the table and across the low cut-glass bowl of delicate white flowers to Francesca, sitting between Pietro and George. Two men with broad shoulders and Italian hair cuts, dark eyes and lightweight suits, but George was almost three-quarters American in manner and speech. From time to time, Theresa dragged her mind away from Hugo who tried to take up her full attention until she hinted that the lady on his other side was being neglected. She saw Pietro's jasper eyes watching her when Francesca talked to George, but he gave no sign of smiling. When Francesca turned to him, her face full of laughter, he softened, bent his head and murmured words that could be heard only by the woman who touched his sleeve with an air of belonging.

The food was exquisite and varied and most of the guests ate and drank the fine wines with enjoyment, but George, after the first show of enthusiasm, picked at his food and pushed away his plate before he had finished, as each course came. He drank wine and water in small quantities and as the evening progressed, became silent, and even Francesca could not make him smile. As they left the table to go for coffee and liqueurs on the wide terrace under the stars, Francesca put a hand on his arm and looked up, with anxiety in her eyes.

'It's all right, honey. Don't fuss. It must be a bug I picked up in Rome.'

'Will you have coffee or shall I order lemon juice?'

He shuddered as he contemplated drinking the Italian cure-all for stomach disorders and Theresa noticed that he held a hand flat on his abdomen as if in pain. He sat quietly sipping mineral water while the conversation flowed round him and Theresa found herself drawn to his side. Francesca looked across and smiled, gratefully. Hugo looked vaguely annoyed when Theresa left him with a murmured apology, but settled down to a long discourse about the sealed artesian wells in Venice, that had been superseded by piped water from terra firma, to help stop the city sinking as the water under the buildings was used up.

'How are you?' said Theresa in a whisper.

'Fine, just fine,' said George. He tried to smile. 'Nice for Franny to have such a good friend,' he said. He paused. 'I was forgetting. You're the girl who treated her sprain. In that pretty get-up, I'd never take you for a medic.'

'I *am* a nurse, George, and you are in pain. Relax and admit it.'

'Thank God for that,' he said. 'Tell you the truth I feel lousy. Can I get out of here?'

'Behind you is the door to the foyer and the toilet. Think you can make it?' she said, briskly.

'Let's go.' He heaved himself to his feet and she took his arm as if they were going to look round the garden. Outside the door, he ran and she waited for him to emerge. She looked at her watch. He had been in there for five minutes. She walked about, trying to look nonchalant. Ten minutes and he was not out. This was worrying and she couldn't very well go into the men's room to find him. A waiter went by but she didn't know how to ask him to look in the room to see if George was all right. Suddenly, the busy hotel seemed empty. She walked twice more up to the door and back. This was stupid. Didn't any of the men in the dining-room need to use the lavatory? The door from the terrace opened and Pietro stood there, looking furious.

She went to him, hurrying, and he caught her by the arm roughly. 'What the hell do you think you are doing? Everyone has noticed that you and George left together and now they are all watching for you to surface. How dare you spoil Francesca's party? How could you cause gossip on this night of all nights?'

'You don't understand. He's in there.'

'He's where?' Pietro stared at the door with the neat illustration of a man on the shining paintwork. 'Not all this time. That's no excuse.' He let her arm fall, his manner less exasperated. 'I suppose he is as much to blame. I warned you that that dress wasn't suitable,' he said, with complete lack of logic and truth.

'If you could stop for one moment and consider me as that nice little thing you like to keep in uniform, perhaps I can tell you,' she said icily. 'George has one big belly-ache and I didn't want him throwing up over Francesca's guests. Does *that* make sense? Better get scrubbed, Doctor. You might have an appendix on your hands! He's in there and *you* can now cope.' She ran back to the terrace and went to Francesca who looked angry and confused. 'George is ill,' she whispered. 'I got him out just in time before he was sick.'

To her surprise, Francesca burst into tears. 'Is that all?' She hugged the surprised girl and kissed her on both cheeks.

'All? He might have a grumbling appendix, or worse.'

'George is strong like an ox. He will be fine.' Francesca seemed back to her normal mood.

'But you were anxious about him.'

'I was anxious about you, *cara*. I saw you leave with him, so close, with arms like so, and I thought that I had kept him waiting too long. I thought you had stolen him from me after all this time. I wanted to kill you,' she added cheerfully. Her face paled. 'But you said he might be ill, really ill? My darling! I must go to him,' she said dramatically and ran from the terrace without any sign of a limp.

Theresa followed, slowly. George and Francesca? Oh, no! If Pietro thought that he was the man that Francesca loved, how would he feel now that Francesca had made public the fact that she and the American planned to marry?

CHAPTER SIX

THE ambulance launch had come quickly, with men in white coats carrying a light stretcher to transfer George Clemente from the Cipriani Hotel to the clinic. In vain, Theresa had protested that she was not needed at the clinic, that Pietro had a full and competent staff and that she was finished with her work in Venice and leaving at the first opportunity.

'You cannot go,' Francesca protested. 'You must stay and look after my Georgio. I know that Pietro wants you and I shall have peace of mind if you are with them, to help and to talk to George when there are only Italian-speaking staff there. He may have had an Italian father but he is American and speaks little Italian. Please, Theresa, for me.'

'You'll have to come,' said Pietro, sharply. 'I can't have you wandering about San Marco looking like that. You can't go back alone in a gondola.'

'I could ask for a water taxi,' she said.

'I had ordered a gondola,' he said, as if that settled the matter. 'And Francesca is very upset. She will feel better if she knows that you are with him.' From the set of his jaw, Theresa knew that he would be very difficult if she refused to go with the ambulance. Soon, she told herself, I shall go away and make decisions for myself once more instead of having them made for me by a chauvinistic Italian. How did I ever think for one moment that he was English? Here, the fact that he had one parent from each country was obscured by the situation in which he worked, the way he lived and the people with whom he mixed.

'How is he? Have you decided what is wrong?' she whispered. He shook his head. 'Have you finished being sick, George?' she said.

'I wasn't sick. I just felt like it. I have this pain. Hell, I feel like a woman in labour.'

'I doubt it,' said Theresa with a smile. 'Try deep breathing. It will help the nausea and relax some of the muscles.' She put a hand on his abdomen and told him to breathe deeply even if it was tender, and to let out the air slowly, so that his muscles couldn't get tense. From the hotel, she had begged a plastic bag of ice and this she laid on his forehead to cool him, placing a small towel under it to take away the first chill. Pietro watched her efforts and when the ambulance was half way across the canal, he came to take her place, letting his hand lie flat on the tense abdomen and pressing very gently. He frowned.

'No positive McBurney.' He felt again, loosening the trousers even more and feeling to one side and lower down. His face showed concern. 'Pass me that ice,' he said, and laid the bag carefully over the spot where he had found the hard mass that was painful. He pushed gently and George gasped his relief as the ice acted as a local anaesthetic and the muscles relaxed.

'What is it, Peter?'

'Suppose you tell me,' said Pietro Bassano. 'You've had this for some time, haven't you?'

George let his head roll to one side on the pillow. 'I never thought it would do this. They said I should have it done last year, but after a holiday from lifting anything heavy, I thought it was better.' He grinned. 'I should have stayed away from the reconstruction work. I heaved a heavy stone from one of the broken pillars and felt something go, but I hoped it would wait.'

'This can't wait, George.' Pietro turned to Theresa. 'I hope you can scrub for a strangulated hernia?'

'I can if I have to,' she said. 'But surely you have all the staff you need?' She gave a slight smile. 'I thought you were a thoracic surgeon. Doesn't that restrict you to everything above the waist?'

'Hey! Stop talking like that. It's my hernia,' said George with a feeble attempt at laughter. 'Ouch!'

'It's all right, George. I did more than my stint as a general surgeon just before I came here.' Pietro Bassano had the grace to blush. 'I admit that I had to pick up anything you could teach me about the theatre arrangements before I could work with my team here. In fact, I couldn't have done any work without you or someone from Mr Nuttall's team,' he said to Theresa.

'And see who you got,' George took her hand. 'Beautiful as well as brainy? It isn't fair.'

'He only needs my brains,' she whispered. 'The other is just a liability.'

George winked. 'Franny told me.'

Told him what? Theresa couldn't understand what he meant, but he was in no fit state now to talk so she held his hand and tried to will him to keep calm although the pain was coming back.

He was taken quickly and without undue disturbance from the ambulance to the clinic. Doors were already open and nurses flitted about the corridor, ready to take him for preparation for operation. 'It must be done now,' said Pietro. 'If we leave it until any food he ate has gone from his stomach, we could have a gangrenous piece of gut on our hands.'

'Who have you worked with in general surgery?' Theresa asked. She gave a sigh of relief when he mentioned a leading surgeon who came to St Edmund's sometimes for private cases, or to assist the surgeon there, when a major case needing two surgeons at the same time was being done. 'I know his work. Have you a set of the clamps he uses?'

'I have my own set in a bag in the theatre. I'll ring them and ask them to put them into the steriliser. I'm glad you reminded me.'

'You use synthetic sutures and fairly small atraumatics for the peritoneum?' He nodded. 'Do you think they should prepare a Paul's tube just in case?'

Once more he nodded. 'I hope it isn't necessary.

The poor blighter is getting married soon and I wouldn't wish open drainage on anyone.' He looked sombre and Theresa wondered if he was concerned not just for his patient, as any responsible doctor would be, but because he had discovered that the woman he loved had been planning to marry another man and would be lost to him.

'You will help me?' She nodded. George had asked her the same question as he was taken away to be shaved and how could she refuse, with the memory of Francesca begging her to stay with George?

'It will be all right,' she said, meaning that he would be able to forget Francesca in time.

'I'm sure it will,' he said, looking at her curiously. 'But it's good to have your unsolicited testimony. I *am* a fairly good surgeon.' He laughed. 'I don't know what the staff here think. The sooner you get out of that lovely garment, the better. Take care to put it somewhere safe while you are here. I want to see it again.'

Her pulse beat faster. Was he at last considering her as a woman to be admired and not just a girl to be taken? 'You may not see it again,' she said. 'Remember, I'm almost on my way home.'

'You have to go to the Nuttall party. I shall see you there,' he said.

'And a hundred others.' She followed the nurse to the room that was becoming familiar, and the dress was put in a cupboard while she put on another of the cotton shifts worn under the theatre gown. The night nurse spoke no English. So much for his promise to have one member of staff to help her, she thought wryly, and then knew she was being unfair. He hadn't expected her to work in the theatre tonight so he couldn't make any arrangements. She went to cupboards, indicating items that might be needed. A nurse wearing a gown much too long for her appeared, and seemed frightened of what might be expected of her, but the senior girl spoke to her and told her to hitch up her gown, or so it seemed to Theresa. They all smiled and shrugged, as if agreeing to do their best and to make the most of whatever skills they had.

One more short wait and the patient was wheeled in, lightly asleep. Pietro passed a laryngoscope, through which the rubber tubing was conducted to the stomach and the contents removed. While this was being done, he scrubbed in the sparkling white bay, and once more his eyes regarded the shrouded figure of the girl who had so recently been dining at the Cipriani, in quite a different gown and with her auburn hair falling in soft curls, almost hiding the tiny earrings.

Theresa looked round the theatre and knew that she was needed. Most of the cases treated at the clinic were booked in with plenty of notice, and the various surgeons and physicians made their own arrangements. As in many English nursing homes and private hospitals, usually a theatre nurse was provided, a senior staff nurse or theatre sister to scrub and assist and the surgeon alerted the anaesthetist, the patient's doctor and perhaps a student or two from the local hospital or a house surgeon. For a case like this, it was also usual to have someone spare to hold retractors, to hang on to clamps or to operate the various suction and diathermy machines, to see that everything needing monitoring was done and that drips and drainage were adequate.

But now there was only one nurse to pick up and check dirty swabs, the anaesthetist and a junior nurse to help him, Pietro Bassano, and Nurse Theresa Callan.

The surgeon looked at her. 'You see, I can't do without you,' he said.

'If I wasn't here, you would have to manage,' she said, 'But it was rather fortunate that we were with George when he collapsed.'

'If you hadn't been here, he would have gone to the hospital. Unless staff come in from outside with the surgeon, night cases are seldom done here.'

Theresa turned to the trolley, pleased, in spite of the fact that she knew he was flattering her, to get her to work for him. 'Is anyone coming to hold a retractor?' she said, knowing that at some point in the operation, it would be very difficult to cope with the instruments and sutures, having to work with one hand while the other held on to a retractor that had a will of its own as the muscles pulled it away from her.

'I hope that someone is coming in about ten minutes. He's finishing a round and checking on the boy with the peach stone in his lung and then he'll help.' He made the first incision, and the next few minutes were busy with the first stages of the operation, minor blood vessels to be tied off, skin clamps to be fixed and sterile towels pinned to the skin edges to make a clean area for surgery. As the scalpel went deeper through the muscle layers, it was a relief to hear the sound of running water in the scrubbing bay and to know that help was coming. The assistant came and muttered a greeting and was soon fully involved. Theresa held ready the swabs needed, firmly clamped into sponge-holding forceps so that they could go deep with them and not lose them. Silk ties threaded through the eye of an aneurysm needle were ready and atraumatic sterile needles and suture material were waiting to sew up the peritoneum. At last, the glistening film that covered the lower intestine was visible and through it Pietro saw the piece of gut tightly caught between two muscle layers.

'What do you think?' he said. Theresa and the assistant peered down into the brightly lit cavity.

'Any pulse?' ventured Theresa, knowing that if the blood supply was cut off completely and the trapped piece had been left for a while, there was a risk that the piece would die and have to be taken out. This would mean a far more extensive operation than just a simple herniotomy to replace the loop of gut in its rightful spot and make sure that the muscle layers were sewn up firmly to stop it coming through again. She handed Pietro a herniotome and he cautiously found a way through the stricture. Once released, the gut regained its colour and blood could be felt pulsing through the blood vessels.

'We're in time,' said Pietro. 'I can do a simple repair without removing anything but the weak hernial sac.'

A lighter atmosphere prevailed and it was possible to talk normally, knowing that George Clemente was a very fortunate man to escape a major operation. With a much lighter heart, she handed him everything he needed and wondered why he was so silent. Usually, once a decision had been made, it was normal for the surgeon to talk if he wanted to do so, but even now, knowing that George would be better in a comparatively short time, Pietro worked quietly as if the result was of no importance. Theresa looked at the side view of the man working with such impersonal care and precision. She couldn't believe that he would wish that the operation had gone badly or the patient's condition should worsen under his care.

'Diathermy on coagulation,' he said quietly, and his tone gave nothing of his private feelings away to the people working with him. Theresa imagined Francesca waiting at the hotel, her face pale and distraught, the picture of a woman worried about the man she loved. Surely Pietro had known that Francesca was in love with George. She glanced at him again as he reached for the needle-holder and skin sutures and her heart ached for him. If he hadn't known until the dinner party who Francesca was going to marry, he must be suffering agonies of mind at this moment, knowing that he was helping her to arrive at the date of her wedding with a man made whole by his rival's care.

'Well, that seems to be all,' said Pietro in a flat voice. He thanked the Italian anaesthetist and his assistant, took off his own mask, smiled at the nurse and looked at Theresa with sombre eyes. 'Thank you, Nurse Callan.' He went into the surgeons' room while the others dressed the incision with a sealing spray then put George back into a theatre gown for his return to the ward.

Slowly, Theresa walked to the changing room, feeling hot and suddenly very tired. She peeled off her shift and showered, and the cool water was wonderful on her hot skin. She dried her body and put on her bra and bikini pants. Now what could she wear? Dawn was well on its way and the silver glints on the water were tinged with pink and blue. She yawned. 'I'll be coming home with the milk,' she murmured. She put on the dress she had worn to the Cipriani and laughed, softly. They'd never believe that she had to go home wearing evening dress while Venice was waking up—not because she had enjoyed a romantic interlude with a handsome man, but rather because she had spent most of the night in a room smelling of disinfectant while her escort operated on another man's internal organs!

She combed her hair, pushing it back from her

face in damp wisps, and found a lipstick which was all she had with her for use at the Cipriani. It's been useful, she recalled, as she outlined the gentle line of her mouth. I've had to use it twice for Pietro Bassano. She smudged it and had to begin again. The thought of Pietro with her lipstick on his face was enough to make her tremble. The memory of his arms and kisses were enough to make her weep. She firmly applied the colour again and heard a tap on the door. The little nurse held out a note. Theresa turned it over and saw that the nurse expected a reply.

'Can you be ready in ten minutes? Francesca rang and asked for you. She won't believe me when I tell her that George is all right. So, Nurse Callan, you can't catch a plane before breakfast.'

'A water taxi is coming,' said Pietro. He regarded her with one eyebrow raised. 'I forgot that you were wearing that dress.'

'It's all I have with me,' she said. 'Can I go straight back to the Danieli? It's still very early and not many people will see me.'

He frowned. 'Not the best way to return after a night out.'

'I might have been dancing all night,' she said. 'That does happen sometimes, I suppose? Every time a girl comes back late, it can't be that she has been peering into someone's peritoneum.' She said it hoping that he would laugh but he looked stern.

'If I go back now, I can slip in and up the stairs quickly.'

'And into the suite? I think not. I have to see Francesca and I want you with me. It would be better if you come with me,' he said, firmly.

'I could go back alone and change, take the next water taxi and be with you in an hour.' She saw that he wore cotton trousers and a blue cotton shirt. 'It's all right for you. You have rooms here and I assume clothes? Would you want to appear at the Cipriani for breakfast in evening dress?'

'No, of course not, but I don't want you going back to the hotel unescorted.'

'I can look after myself,' she said. 'I go everywhere I want to at home without anyone thinking I can't look after myself,' she began.

'But not here. Come with me.'

They reached the penthouse suite of a small block behind the main building, hidden from the canal by the high wall that had once contained an orchard. He unlocked a door and she found herself in a large room with windows overlooking a small canal and a tiny bridge, over which she could see glimpses of the main waterway with boats and gondolas moored by the various buildings. It was peaceful, and speckled light fell on the water through the lattice of wisteria.

'It's lovely,' she said, spontaneously. 'Is this your apartment?' He nodded and went to another room which held a wide bed covered with a dark blue silk cover. The white carpet was thick but gave an illusion of deep coolness, echoed in the pale walls and well-chosen furnishings.

He flung open a wardrobe that occupied the whole of one wall. At one end was a collection of suits and shirts that must belong to him. At the other end were dresses, trousers, jackets, all new, all of the latest designs, separated from his things by a partition. She stared, first at the clothes and then at his impassive face. It was a shock but one that she should have expected. What wealthy Italian man would have a suite of rooms like this with no mistress or wife to grace it?

He reached inside and selected a simple dress of turquoise silk with a fitted bodice and slender shoulder straps that would look equally good in the sun or in a smart hotel. 'Try that,' he said and left her to dress.

She fingered the fabric, which was pure silk. It fitted well and she carefully rolled the other dress and put it in a large plastic bag. It was almost like being in a shop. But what woman, however fond of new clothes, and however predatory, would have such a vast number of new clothes at one time?

'I was right. It fits,' he said as she went out into the huge sitting-room again. 'It also goes well with your accessories.' He gave a crooked smile. 'What Englishman would know or care about such things? What American?'

She smiled, gently. It had been on the tip of her tongue to say she couldn't wear it as it belonged to someone who might well object to her clothes being

lent to a stranger in this arbitrary manner. His sad
eyes had stopped her. He was suffering because he
had to see Francesca with the news that her wedding plans need not be postponed. He must eat
breakfast with her, knowing that he was not the
man of her choice, and try to live with that knowledge.

'It's beautiful. If you are sure the owner won't
mind, I shall love wearing it. It is more suitable than
the other one.' She laughed. 'I felt as if someone
might burst into song if I climbed out of a gondola
wearing that at six in the morning, like they did in
the old Hollywood musicals. I once saw a reissue of
one and they sang "Broadway Melody". Have you
heard it?'

He shook his head. 'You must sing it for me,' he
said, politely. 'Now, we must go. Leave that here.'
He indicated the other dress. 'I hate to be weighed
down with parcels and you'd probably leave it in
the taxi.'

Obediently, she left it on a chair and he locked
the door of the suite as they closed the door behind
them. A very private place for which there might be
two keys? She wondered who the other woman
was. Someone of her size, if this one dress was any
guide. Someone young who liked good colours.
She frowned. Some had been out of character with
the woman she imagined wearing them. She shrugged. We all make mistakes sometimes, she
thought. But to buy several dresses that didn't suit
must be a very costly mistake. It was difficult to

guess sizes when garments were still on hangers in a row, but some had seemed larger than the one that she was now wearing and of a style that wouldn't suit her. It was as if the owner had dressed in a fairly restrained way, in dull colours, when she was fatter, and had burst out into younger, brighter dresses as she lost weight. It couldn't be Francesca. Her bone structure was such that her weight would be constant—she might even weigh the same now as she had five years ago, able to use the same measurements for everything she wore.

One last telephone call and Pietro was ready, his dark eyes giving away nothing of what he might be feeling. He helped Theresa down into the taxi with care, making her wonder if he was secretly concerned that she should not soil the beautiful silk dress that she wore. She tried to make a mental joke of the whole business. What if they met his mistress at the hotel? I shall know if a woman glares at me and asks where I bought my dress, she thought. It was exclusive enough to be a model, and would annoy any woman who thought it was the only one in circulation.

The canal was quiet and a softness of air and colour told that dawn had only just decided to appear. The morning was young and innocent and Theresa had that fragile wakefulness that comes after a night of work and no rest, with the sudden coming of day. She was also very hungry. A glance at her watch told her that it was much too early for breakfast and even if Francesca had waited up for news of George, the chances were that now she was resting.

Pietro also glanced at his watch. He looked at his companion and grinned more normally, and suddenly more English. 'We can't wait for Francesca,' he said. 'We'll have some food before I let her know we've arrived.'

'Isn't she expecting to breakfast with us?'

'I can eat two, and I'm sure you can drink some more coffee when she comes down.' He led her to a small terrace away from the main restaurant and the waiter showed no surprise at being asked for breakfast at six-thirty in the morning. Theresa recalled that scheduled air flights sometimes made early or very late meals necessary and when she heard the drone of an aircraft coming in to land at the distant airport, she wondered when she would be ready to leave for England. Each day so far, something had happened to keep her in Venice, in spite of Pietro Bassano saying so firmly when she arrived that she should go home at once. He had been the one to keep her, even when he seemed to dislike her, to distrust her reactions to men like Luigi and to resent her attractive appearance as a threat to his peace of mind and his reputation.

The coffee was hot and very black, the cream cold and thick. Fresh bread and cherry preserve came with butter in cut-glass dishes filled with chips of ice. Theresa refused eggs but watched Pietro eat with all the enjoyment of a ten-year-old boy. Her heart was warm with love for him and yet she had to close her mind to any thoughts of sharing breakfast with him under other circumstances. He was in love with Francesca, although he was hiding it very well as he ate and drank in the early sunshine. A man who had to hide cold facts from patients must have the self-discipline to hide his own emotions and he was doing it well.

Theresa frowned. The Italian side of his nature might make it easier. She had seen for herself that he took another kind of interest in women. His sudden, almost uncontrollable need of her as a sex object was a memory she would rather forget, finding it difficult to equate it with the relaxed and very attractive man who was scraping the last sticky remnants of the cherry preserve on to another bread roll. And there were the clothes she had seen in the closet of the impressive penthouse apartment on top of the clinic. To have all those beautiful couturier dresses and suits in one place, divided from his clothes only by a wooden partition, meant that whoever owned them had not stayed for just an overnight visit! It suggested permanence and continuity of an arrangement that couldn't be wholly a business affair.

She bit her lip. What kind of an affair was it? Because he loved Francesca, he couldn't be deeply in love with this other woman. He was so scathing about Luigi and yet he was carrying on in the same way, being a complete hypocrite. All that pious reference to reputation was insincere, a cover up for a way of living that Theresa found distasteful and in which she wanted no part. She glanced at him. If only I didn't want him, love him and ache for him as I do, it would be easy to get on the next plane back to England and take up another job with a patient who needed real nursing care.

'That's better,' he said, and smiled the kind of smile that made her want to weep with frustration and anger. How could any man who looked as he did in the early morning, be as wicked and as devious as she knew him to be?

'Yes, I feel more human,' she said.

'Not too human, I hope.' He smiled again but with the caution of someone about to make an unwelcome remark. 'Luigi is back for a day or so and I have to be at the clinic this afternoon.'

'That doesn't concern me,' she said.

'He will be working in the suite this afternoon. I don't think you should be there.'

'I shall sleep this afternoon,' she said. 'I have a lot of rest to make up. You look fresh but my eyes feel gritty from lack of sleep.' He opened his mouth to speak but she continued quickly. 'Talking of eyes. You seem perfectly all right. No signs of infection. I'd better put in some more drops if we have time before Francesca comes to breakfast, and then, if you hear that the path. report is clear, I think we could stop the treatment, don't you?' She rummaged in her holdall for the box containing the drops and swabs. 'There isn't a soul about so I can do them here if you like,' she said.

'Very well.' Obediently he sat with his back to

the light and tilted his head backwards so that she could look into his eyes. Briskly but gently, she instilled the drops and mopped up the residue. 'Thank you,' he said formally. 'Theresa.'

'Yes?' she said.

'I think you were telling me politely to mind my own business.' She blushed. 'But I do know Luigi and I do know that here, away from your normal surroundings, you could be in danger from men who want to take advantage of your beauty, your youth and freshness, and your ingenuous expression.'

'I'm tougher than I look,' she said.

'I know that. I also know that you are either deeply in love with someone and have no inclination to go with a lover, or . . .'

'Pietro, darling!' Francesca came towards them slowly, her face anxious and her steps unwilling to take her to the man who might have bad news for her. To Theresa, it seemed that she was cautious, not because she was worried about George, but because she knew that Pietro would realise that she had deceived him, using him as a front behind which she could pursue her love for the American.

He went to her and the cold fingers of loneliness once more traced a wall round Theresa's heart. He took the slender fingers in both of his hands and kissed them. 'It will be all right,' he said. Francesca burst into tears. Her head was cradled against the firm chest and his fingers caressed her hair as he murmured words of comfort in Italian. Theresa beckoned to the waiter and ordered more coffee and whatever Signorina Vidali ate for breakfast. It gave her something to do so that the sight of the two people need not make her want to cry too.

'And you came too, to tell me. It is kind. I need to be told the truth and I was afraid that if it was bad, Pietro would not tell me.' Francesca smiled. 'He has a soft heart and does not like to give pain.'

'George is going to be quite well in a very short time,' said Theresa. 'We were worried, but Pietro was in time and an hour made all the difference.'

'But you knew how ill he was and made him admit it. I shall remember that when we are married and this anxious time has been lost in the years.'

'You may see him later today, Francesca, but you must not stay for long. You may not want to stay for more than a few minutes as George will be feeling very sorry for himself and won't look his best.' He smiled to take away the implication that the man she loved was really ill. 'I'll collect you about four o'clock,' he added.

'And Theresa? You will come with me? I am afraid of such places and I need you with me.'

'No, Theresa will be resting.' He sounded as if he had been the one to order her to rest in the suite. What had made him change his mind about her ability to keep Luigi at bay? 'But if you come back to the Danieli, you could eat with us. Luigi will be there and we can make up a small party,' he said.

'Dear Luigi. So wicked, but so good,' said Francesca.

Theresa smiled, slightly. So even the beautiful Francesca accepted that the handsome Italian was attractive. Perhaps she knew more about his amorous behaviour than her light remarks suggested. The fact that she was in love with George while clinging to Pietro in such a possessive manner, indicated that she was not averse to having handsome men firmly on the end of silken strings for her own amusement. But it was impossible to dislike her. I must have had a very sheltered life, Theresa thought. Everyone here seems to take it for granted that love is a very trivial thing, except for this latest love of Francesca's. Her love for George was real, accentuated by the sudden shock of his collapse.

Pietro was smiling and pouring fresh coffee into three cups. How controlled he must be to accept that the love he wanted was given to another man. Nothing in his manner showed the dismay and jealousy he must now feel. He saw Francesca regarding the silk dress with a puzzled frown. She looked at him as if to ask a question. 'You recognise it?' he said.

She smiled, rather archly. 'Very nice. Very suitable. And the others?'

He laughed. 'They are still there, but I could see that you recognised this dress.'

'Does Selina know?'

'Not yet,' he shrugged. 'I hope she will not notice until I tell her. She comes back tonight, I believe.'

If they had been talking in Italian, Theresa could have sat and watched the sunlight on the water and listened to the evocative sighing of boats passing the hotel and making small waves on to the landing stage, but as they sat there, talking over her head, she knew how a ghost must feel, who is discussed and not seen by the people round it. I'm here, she wanted to shout. Remember me? I'm the girl who is used and then put on a velvet chair until required again in the operating theatre!

'If Francesca has finished with me, I think I'll get back to the Danieli,' she said. They looked surprised. 'I have a lot to do,' she said. 'I think my work here has been done and I shall pack and enquire about planes.' Her voice was steady as she asked, 'What shall I do with the dress? Do I send it to the cleaner?'

'Keep it,' said Pietro. 'There are plenty more where that came from.'

Theresa smiled through frozen lips. 'Thank you,' she said. 'It will make a special kind of souvenir.'

'Promise me we'll meet for dinner again tonight before you make final plans,' said Francesca, with a quick glance at the suddenly expressionless face of the man with them.

'I . . . all right, Francesca, I'll wait until I know how George is and I'll see you this evening.'

She made her escape, aware of the dark eyes watching her retreat. Was it a retreat? Her shoulders sagged as she waited for the water bus to take her back to San Marco. It was a cowardly escape from a situation that both fascinated her and sickened her. 'Plenty more where that came from'. And plenty more girls who would give themselves for a rail of new dresses. 'Well, I'm not one,' she said, to the amazement of a huge woman in black who thought she must have stepped on the feet of the pretty woman with the angry green eyes.

'*Scusi, Signorina,*' she said as Theresa stepped from the boat.

CHAPTER SEVEN

As SHE turned the key in the lock, Theresa heard voices. She gave a sigh of relief. It was one thing to be independent and to state so firmly that she could look after herself. But she had braced herself as if for a physical assault as soon as she passed under the elaborate chandeliers in the corridor of the Danieli Hotel where the suite of rooms was situated. If Luigi was there, talking, he couldn't exactly make a grab at her as she went to her room.

'Hugo!' Her pleasure was real as she saw the American who had dined with them on the evening when George was taken ill.

'Hello, honey. How is he?' The huge hands once more enveloped her fingers with warmth and friendliness.

'George? He's fine, or will be once he gets over today. He is sore and a bit resentful at having tubes in his arm and stomach, but he should lose those in a day or so.'

'That's fine.' His eyes took in the details of her smart dress. 'And you helped with all that! I just can't believe it. You're such a little doll, it doesn't seem right.'

'Really Hugo, times have changed since women were expected to sit at home and do the bidding of their husbands, only taken down from the shelf and dusted whenever they were needed on view or for sex. We work, these days, us dolls,' she said, laughing, but seeing that Luigi took in everything.

'You sound a little bit put out. Tired?' Hugo was immediately concerned. 'Can I get you something. It's early, but a little pick-me-up?'

'Nothing, thank you. I am tired and I intend sleeping for a while.' Luigi brightened and she wondered what he had in mind for her once the protective American left the suite. She smiled, sweetly. 'Are you going to be here later? Pietro is taking Francesca to see George this afternoon once it is cooler and then coming here to eat tonight.'

'That sounds great. Mind if I join you?'

'I'll look forward to it. They will have the latest news about him. Would you like to order some tea and come at the same time—about six? I'd rather have that than a cocktail, but you order what you want.'

Luigi looked angry. 'If you sleep, I cannot work.'

'Of course you can. Didn't Pietro say that you had a desk in your own room and everything you needed?' She smiled. 'I believe that Francesca is expecting to see you at dinner, too, Luigi. Quite a party,' she added.

There would be safety in a group. Hugo, blessed man, would be her friend and would never do anything to annoy her or to suggest any form of sexual harassment. 'If you'll excuse me,' she said, sweetly. 'Perhaps if you telephone the clinic and tell Pietro that you will be here this evening, he can fix the time.'

'That's a great idea. Perhaps they will know of a girl for Luigi to make up the party,' Hugo said.

Theresa went into their room, laughing as she locked the door. Poor Luigi, to be the odd one in a party and the man for whom a spare girl must be found! She put the silk dress on a hanger and lay on the bed in her underwear. The soft filtered light came through the blinds and the sounds from outside were muffled and comforting. Once or twice, she heard the siren of a vessel going from the liner dock to Yugoslavia and she rested in a half-sleep of dreams and imaginings that were both sad and gentle. Pietro's face seemed to haunt her even now in the darkened room. It was a face showing so many varied moods, such strength and honesty written on the clear brows that she couldn't believe that he was a monster, taking his pleasure from women as and when he wanted them and leaving a trail of wounded hearts behind him.

She fought sleep, hearing Luigi moving about rather like a prowling lion, but she was safe in her room and her heavy eyelids refused to stay open.

She woke with the question in her mind that had been there when she slipped into oblivion. He had said . . . what had he said when she was with him at the Cipriani, waiting for Francesca? That Theresa was either deeply in love with someone and so not inclined to have a lover, or . . . She frowned, her wits gathering again. He hadn't finished what he was saying as Francesca had come towards them, wanting news of George. Was he accusing her of being frigid, lacking the warm sexual urges that normal women possessed? Was it his way of saying she was virtuous only because she was frigid and not because of any moral beliefs?

Theresa thought back to her early days as a student nurse. She had encountered that kind of moral blackmail when a student with innocent blue eyes had assured her that she would sleep with him unless she was frigid. She liked him, didn't she? She wanted love and he could supply that need. She had resisted it then and found that he tried it on with any pretty girl he met, with varying success. Had Pietro been about to sink as low? She heard voices outside and knew it was safe to go across to the bathroom for a shower. She took her clothes with her and tied the belt of her kimono firmly round her waist, enjoying the furious glance from Luigi as Hugo merely smiled and settled his bulky frame into a chair to wait for her before having tea.

As she passed the American, he winked, solemnly, behind Luigi's back, and Theresa had the sudden thought that Hugo was not there by accident, but was extending the chaperon's duties imposed by Pietro Bassano. She didn't know if she was annoyed or not, but in fairness, decided that she had been very glad to see him when she first came to the suite that morning. She breathed deeply, feeling refreshed and back to normal.

When she poured tea for the men, she was cool

and trim in the silky coffee-coloured dress she had worn on the day of the funeral, brightened with cream belt and shoes and a chiffon scarf of pale green. The pure silk dress from the penthouse was hanging in her wardrobe, where, she assured herself, it would remain until it was packed and taken to England as a sobering reminder that Italian men were wonderful, handsome, attractive and completely heartless.

'I got in touch,' said Hugo, gulping his tea and reaching for a cream cake. 'Peter said OK and will we be in the bar at eight?' He filled his mouth again and they waited for him to continue. 'Know anyone called Selina?' he asked Luigi.

Tea slopped in the saucer and Theresa tried to mop it up without them seeing it, using a tissue. Her first thought was that the woman would appear in the doorway, demanding her dress and making a scene as she took it for granted that Theresa was a new light-of-love.

'Selina? Is she in Venice?' Luigi looked interested.

'Yeah. Peter said she's here for a few days and flying out soon, so we're lucky to date her. She's coming to make up the party. Said she'd be pleased to partner you, Luigi.'

Lucky to be able to date her? Was her appointment book so full? Perhaps she was a professional, a kind of high-class tart who obliged certain gentlemen when she was in Venice. Theresa filled the cups again and hoped that she had kept her cool. A spark of mischief took over. I'll be able to observe and be objective, she thought. It might be a situation both amusing and poignant. She thought of the Venetian masks she had seen in the craftsman's shop. I shall feel as if I am wearing a mask, and so will Pietro. Under those masks, our hearts may be breaking, but on the shining surface, we shall be amusing, friendly and enjoy the evening and the company. And I'm dying to see the competition, she admitted to herself.

The house phone trilled. It was Pietro, to say that Francesca would be arriving in ten minutes with Selina. Could Hugo and Theresa come down to wait for them while he changed? 'Be right there,' said Hugo, who had answered the telephone. Theresa noticed with amusement that Luigi had vanished into the bathroom and was giving a passionate rendering of an aria from Puccini as he splashed and beautified himself for Selina. It could have been me, she thought, with a chuckle.

'Useful girl, Selina,' said Hugo with another knowing wink. 'Got him out of your hair, didn't it?'

'You are a cunning devil,' said Theresa, affectionately. 'I'm very grateful for your company today.'

'My pleasure. Always did like a pretty girl, and what he said is right.'

'What who said?'

'Ready? Come on then, girl, we haven't all night,' he growled, with a smile. 'Let's leave loverboy to pat on the cologne.' They walked along to the lift and Theresa wondered what it must be like to be loved by someone like Hugo. Life would be comfortable and full of affection, protected and free from worry—and boring.

Her heart beat faster as they nearly collided with Pietro coming along the corridor from the lift. Surely comfort and affection would do instead of this restless passion, this uncertainty that threatened to engulf her. I have no pride, she decided. In my heart, I know that I want to go to him under any circumstances, on whatever terms he offers or does not offer. To be near him was agony and exquisite joy, to touch him was wonderful, and to give herself to him completely would be heaven and hell.

He murmured an apology, touched her arm briefly in passing and went on to the suite of rooms. Hugo pressed the button of the lift and watched the red light flicker on the scale until it rested on the indicator for their floor. It had been in this lift that Pietro Bassano had kissed her in anger and frustration and since then she had avoided using it. Hugo looked benevolent and safe. The lift was lined with the same green velvet and this was still Venice, but the memory of that kiss still electrified the air for her.

Francesca was coming through the main entrance as they reached Reception and Hugo went forward to greet her. Behind her was a blonde girl with a wide and pretty mouth and, Theresa had to admit, big blue eyes full of humour and warmth.

Her figure was good and she wore a pale blue jump-suit slashed almost to the navel, but concealing her shapely bosom in a tantalising way. Luigi will be enchanted, Theresa thought, and knew that he would have eyes for no other woman in the dining-room while Selina was there. And she will need humour if he attacks her with his usual fervour, she thought.

'I saw Georgio,' said Francesca, triumphantly. 'He looks terrible.' She put up her hands, smiling. 'So awful that I must marry him quickly and take care of him.'

'I'm glad. When is it to be?'

'Pietro says we must wait for a little while, but not so very long, I think.' Theresa had the feeling that Francesca would marry George when and where she liked and Pietro would be powerless to protest.

'You'll let him get on his feet first, I hope?'

'George will be better soon,' Francesca said, nodding her head. 'He wishes to see you, Theresa. Can you go tomorrow?'

'Yes, I intend to visit him before I go back to England.'

'You must stay. There is no need for you to go now. You have a room and a holiday before you begin your other boring job and I want you here. Pietro needs you,' she said plaintively.

'He does not.' Theresa refused to be persuaded. 'I have to go back. I have other people to see before I go to Charlotte's.'

'But I thought you were here to help Pietro.'

'I came to nurse Sir Julian and I stayed to help with one or two cases. I have done all I can and now I feel it is time to go.'

'Why, *mia cara*?' The voice was gentle. 'I hope very much that you are not in love with a man at, where is this place with all the babies, Charlotte's?'

'I haven't been there yet.' Theresa, for once, was glad to see Luigi, making it unnecessary for her to have to hide the fact that she *was* in love, but not with an English obstetrician. Luigi was dazzling, in white from head to feet, the sharp crease of his trousers a wonder of pressing. His slim hips snaked towards them, and the gleam of his smile was only slightly less brilliant than the rest of his appearance. Selina eyed him with amusement. She put her head forward, lips pursed. He looked puzzled, and then down into her cleavage.

'You can't embrace me, *caro*,' she said. 'It will crease you too much. You are much too pretty tonight.' He kissed her mouth and then caught her hand, murmuring that he could take the suit off whenever she wished.

Francesca laughed. 'Selina is here for only a short while. She has other commitments, so we must enjoy her company, and you, Luigi, will have to be patient.'

Was Francesca blind? Surely she must know that this was the girl who lived in the penthouse? In fact, Theresa recalled her talking about her to Pietro. I shall never understand what goes on in these beautiful Venetian heads, she thought, so I might as well just enjoy the champagne life while I can. If I stayed here long enough, I might develop the same philosophy of life, but I don't think I want to do so.

Pietro came in almost unnoticed, except by the girl who was waiting for his face, his voice, his dominating presence. Her heart beat faster as she saw that he wore a silk shirt of the same colour as her dress, with dark slim-fitting trousers that made Luigi's figure effeminate in comparison. It had to be coincidence that he had chosen the same colour, but it made them seem a couple rather than two people who happened to be dining in the same party. Francesca called for dry Martinis and the party settled down into talking couples. It was a foregone conclusion that Selina should be with Luigi, who was completely fascinated by her eyes and low-cut revealing neckline, but when Theresa looked up from her drink, she saw her friend and ally, Hugo, in deep conversation with Francesca, which left her no alternative but to stay where she was and watch Pietro walk slowly towards her. Poor man, she thought, with some amusement. His true love is talking to George's friend and probably discussing her future marriage to the American. Selina, who must be Pietro's mistress, was revelling in teasing the handsome Luigi, and he was left with a girl wearing a very plain dress, sitting with her feet demurely together, showing only her lower legs and certainly no hint of thigh or bosom to make the view interesting.

'Is George better?' she asked as he sat down by her side and stretched out his long legs over the deep carpet. A breeze from the water caught his hair and ruffled it slightly. He brushed it back impatiently, as if making a mental note that he should have it cut shorter, but his eyes held none of the censorious expression to which she had become accustomed.

'George is as strong as a horse, and, if we allowed it, he would be eating like one already.'

'Men can be such babies over their treatment,' she said with a wry smile. 'The bigger they are, the worse it is. Usually, if they are fairly dominant, they find it difficult to accept the opinion of others, and as for obeying orders about diet or when it is safe to get out of bed and walk, they are quite difficult.'

'I thought I was very good when you deluged me with saline solution.'

'That's because you knew the dangers of leaving infected discharge in your eyes.' She glanced up, sharply, with professional concern. His eyes were clear and dark with healthy white sclera. She blushed when she saw him staring at her. 'They look healthy enough now,' she said.

'Is that the only time you find it interesting to gaze into the eyes of a man, Theresa? I suppose I should be flattered that you take such an interest in my well-being, but it might be more thrilling if I didn't have the conviction that I know exactly what you are thinking when you look at me.'

She looked away, her thick eyelashes veiling troubled eyes. 'It's a habit of our trade,' she said, lightly. 'When I first went to St Edmund's I sat on buses, quite sure that I knew what was wrong with most of the passengers. I don't think they would have been pleased at many of my diagnoses.'

He laughed. 'You too? I almost asked them if they had made appointments with consultants and found it hard to leave them to their fate. I could have run my own clinic then, with greater conviction than I have had since qualifying. The more one learns, the less sure of the right diagnosis one can be. Sometimes, a patient complains of symptoms and they bear little relationship to the real trouble. I often think we should learn more basic psychology before we are loosed on the unsuspecting world of the sick. So many diseases are psychosomatic in origin and we waste time treating symptoms, yet if we took the time to talk, we could sort out the underlying worry that causes physical pain.

'Not true in most of your cases, I would think,' she said.

'We just don't know. If people hold in emotions, they breathe badly. That becomes a habit and their lungs are never fully extended. Couldn't that lead to many conditions? We know that stress causes heart attacks, but we don't get the patient early enough to treat the stress.' He paused and she glanced up again. 'We can't treat all heart conditions. We talk of the heart being merely a pump, but, in my opinion, the diagnosis of a broken heart still signifies.' His mouth was firm and serious and his eyes were no longer laughing.

'And what is the treatment, Doctor?' she said, breathing fast and trying to appear nonchalant. She saw Francesca laughing with all the innocence of a child. How could she act like that in the same room as the man she had encouraged to love her, and had now betrayed.

'It's a lengthy process, isn't it, Theresa?'

She almost crushed the stem of her glass in her tense fingers. 'How do you know?' she breathed. Just when she was sure that he had no inkling of her feelings towards him, he was telling her that he knew she loved him. It put her once more in his power, knowing that if he touched her or made any advances towards her, she would give in to him, her careful defences crumbling like sand.

'How did I know?' He looked puzzled. 'I assume that you have met such cases. They don't recover physically until they find another partner, fall in love again and forget that, for them, there had been just one person to love.' He leaned forward. 'We know so little of other people's minds.' His dark eyes searched her green eyes. 'When we work together, I think that we might have a genuine rapport, but after the clinic I sense the barrier between us. If it is because I kissed you and offended you, I'm sorry. I had no idea that you were in love with someone.'

'And now?'

'I know that somewhere there is a man who is everything to you and so I promise, that if you come to live at the clinic, I will make no demands on you that have anything to do with your private life or feelings.' He grinned. 'I don't say that it will be easy, but I value your assistance too much to lose you in that capacity.'

She felt sick. He was being understanding and correct in his behaviour so that she would work for him again. His gentle glances, his smiles and his consideration were only a front behind which he was calculating the next thorocoplasty, the next open heart case or the smooth running of his theatre. Of course he had to reassure her that he had no sexual intentions so that she would go to him in all innocence, with complete trust. Come into my parlour, said the spider to the fly! She recalled the full row of dresses in his bedroom, and decided that she didn't need any more new clothes.

'I have to go back soon,' she said, and watched his face set and the dark eyes grow bleak.

'He must be very dear to you,' he said.

'So you have decided that I am capable of love,' she said. 'But in the Cipriani, you said that I was either so much in love that I didn't have time for a lover, or some other reason that you didn't have time to mention.'

He gave her a long cool look that made her feel as if he had stripped her of the demure dress and raked her body with his abrasive glance. The passion was still there, hidden by a thin fragile veil. She fought against her panic and quickening pulse and was thankful to hear Francesca's bird-like voice calling them to the restaurant.

'You must eat. I suppose you talk of people and nasty diseases. I cannot listen now that my Georgio is a patient.'

Luigi and Selina were already seated and talking animatedly. Francesca still monopolised Hugo, as if he brought with him a piece of George to comfort her in her loneliness. Pietro had been stopped once more from telling her that she was lacking in something vital to a sensual relationship and Theresa breathed again. It was stupid to goad him into saying something that must hurt her. Let it go and hope that he forgot that she had recalled the conversation in the Cipriani.

The candle lamps were softly pink and orange, and the faces of the diners took on a misty quality that was flattering and magical. Pietro's hand was on the table, toying with the fine silver fork, just a few inches away from her hand which held the glass of *acqua minerale* that she was drinking. To touch him would do nothing to assuage the fire that smouldered under her skin, but she deliberately let her hand brush against his, only to feel him draw away from her, without a change of expression. To her, the touch had been vibrant with awareness, and it was impossible to think that he had noticed nothing, or, if he had, that he was so unmoved that he could put down his fork and begin to crumble a bread-roll.

The food was deliciously light and refreshing, the wine deceptively mild to drink but mellowing in its effect. Luigi was slightly owl-eyed before the meal was over, and Selina looked even more alluring as her eyes shone with laughter and wine. At least it proves that although he would take me if he could, as he would take any pretty girl, it is a passion that can be switched on and off to suit the occasion. And this dinner party is one occasion when I leave him cold, thought Theresa, bitterly. A quick grab in a lift and a kiss stolen because there was a slight possibility that someone might come, which added to the pleasure, were the limits of his interest. Now that Luigi was fully occupied and no threat to her, Pietro had no need to be attentive, and when they left the table to have coffee on the balcony, Theresa managed to be with Hugo and to leave Pietro to listen to Francesca and her plans for the future.

Theresa watched the glittering water beyond the broad walk in front of the hotel. 'Come on,' Hugo said. 'It's beautiful out there. Why are we sitting here when we have the whole of Venice to explore?'

'Why, indeed?' Francesca rose and assured everyone that her ankle was quite better. 'I shall enjoying walking in San Marco,' she said. 'We can have more coffee later if you wish before I go back to my hotel.'

'I ought to pack,' said Selina. 'I go away the day after tomorrow and I have things to do.'

'I will come with you,' said Luigi, to the surprise of no one, least of all Selina. 'Wait for me,' he said. He went back to the suite and Theresa smiled when he came down with a small case in his hand. It was obvious that he would be staying the night once he had taken Selina home.

'Do you live in Venice?' said Hugo.

Selina shrugged. 'Here and there. I have a very pleasant room now behind the Accademia, near the clinic where Pietro operates.' She smiled ruefully. 'I did have a very nice pad but it was needed for someone and as I am away for much of the year it wasn't reasonable to expect it to be reserved for me all the time.'

And I know where that was, thought Theresa. Did the new clothes go with her, or were the varying sizes and styles ready for whoever came, on the premise that something must fit? Would she take what she wanted and leave the rest for the next gullible creature to share his bed? In her mind, Theresa saw the heavy dark blue silk of the bedcover slide back to reveal the huge king-sized bed that was certainly far too big for one person. Selina seemed to have no regrets, no resentment. If she was used to sleeping around, that must be part of her philosophy—to be loved and left and have no hard feelings.

Selina gave Hugo a peck on the cheek and then turned to Pietro, addressing him in Italian and flinging her arms round his neck to kiss him good-bye. It was the only time that she had looked Italian, and Theresa was mildly surprised to see it, even though Francesca had said that Selina was Italian-Swiss but had worked in many of the capitals of Europe. It was hinted that she had something to do with modelling, but Theresa couldn't decide whether she modelled for Francesca's firm or was free-lance, or even if the title, model, was a courtesy title for her other more interesting activities.

Francesca gathered her shawl over one arm and Hugo gallantly offered his broad wrist to support her hand. Theresa followed, with Pietro looming over her like a shadow. They were silent as they walked out into the Venetian night. If only she could be with him as his lover or his wife, Venice would be heavenly. The gold of the lions of San Marco were hidden in the dusk, but the perfect symmetry of the dark shapes that outlined the Doge's Palace spoke of a time when money and taste and ingenuity ruled the building of such places. Here was dignity and loveliness, taken for granted perhaps by the people who had been born and brought up in such unique surroundings, but a wonder to the rest of the world.

The pigeons had long ago gone to roost, and the bright lights of the cafés now dominated the square. I shall go back to England the first visitor to Venice to leave without seeing the interior of a single church or palazzo—if she could discount the palazzo that was now a clinic—she thought. I haven't been to S. Georgio Maggiore to climb the bell tower, I haven't crossed the Bridge of Sighs and I have only once glimpsed the Rialto Bridge when Pietro took me to dinner, so long ago. With a sense of shock she realised that she had been in Venice for only a week, and yet everything that had happened before Venice had gone into the crevasse that held all past memories. It was impossible to believe that once she was back in England this place would become unreal in its turn and she would wonder if she had really been there.

'I must buy another souvenir before I go back,' she said.

'Do you need that to remember this place?' said Pietro.

'For a friend,' she said, defensively, avoiding his question, and deliberately bought a piece of glass that would do for Sister Pomery when they met again at the party.

They went back, as Francesca was tired. Hugo helped her to the launch that came from the Cipriani to collect them and Theresa waved them away across the dark water, listening to the mournful cry of a gondolier warning of his approach as he paused by a side canal. It was a cry that told her it was time for her to leave Venice. Here there was no life for her that could be bearable. Better to cut her losses and go back to sanity.

They went into the brightly-lit foyer. On the desk was a large envelope addressed to Signorina Callan. She picked it up, ignoring the slightly quizzical frown of her companion. It was her air ticket and itinerary for her return to England, the day after tomorrow. No, that would be tomorrow! The ornate clock in the bell tower struck twelve. She had so little time left to do anything more.

'I have my tickets,' she said, and found that Pietro had gone. He was speaking on the telephone and even though she couldn't see his face, she sensed his tension. He turned, and his face was pale in the reflection from the glittering chandelier. 'What is it?' she asked.

'The boy with the peach stone. One lung has collapsed and we must get over there at once.'

CHAPTER EIGHT

WOULD this weird roundabout of work and high living never settle down to let her go back to a routine that she understood? Theresa tied back her hair and put on a theatre cap. 'We must stop meeting like this,' murmured the doctor assisting Pietro Bassano. She giggled helplessly. If it wasn't so serious, she might have hysterics, but one glance at the thin form on the trolley in the anaesthetic room had killed all her sense of being used, and all sense of anything but the welfare of this poor young body, gasping for breath with pinched blue lips and nose. The oxygen apparatus helped, but he had so little in the way of reserves that all haste was necessary to reverse the shock of a collapsed lung.

'We'll have to take it that the other piece of peach husk that we didn't locate has gone down and made a kind of tumour. He has one lung that works but the shock of his collapse has weakened his pulse and circulation, putting a strain on heart and lungs. We may have to put him on a heart-lung machine, but first we must get on with removing the foreign body.' Pietro had forgotten everything but the boy on the table. 'We have only one heart-lung apparatus here and this is in use. I can't decide on priorities now, so let's see what surgery and careful management can do.' He glanced at the trolleys and grunted. 'Ready to start?'

The flow of oxygen was stepped up and the relaxant that made a deep anaesthesia unnecessary was given. Once more, the theatre was in action. It crossed Theresa's mind that the boy was from a simple family possibly spending their life savings on this expensive time in a private hospital, but she gathered from remarks between the assistant and the anaesthetist when she asked about him, that no fee was being charged as the family had once worked for Pietro. Another side to this strange man who didn't want her but couldn't let her out of his sight.

The boy's colour remained constant but not good. The pleura was tough and Pietro made a careful incision, draining the discharge and sucking out the mass that was causing the trouble. There was no time to X-ray or to do anything more heroic than drain and put in a Tudor-Edward's drainage tube to drain any further discharge.

The dressing was applied and more blood given, the oxygen mask fixed into position while the trolley was wheeled back to the ward with the waiting oxygen tent. 'Crude, but all we could do,' said Pietro. 'The kind of surgery done on the battlefield, but effective, I hope. The lung can expand slowly as the stuff drains and we can control the expansion gradually.'

'Is this to go for study?' said Theresa.

He hesitated, as if he didn't want to know what

the result of the tests would be. 'Yes, it should go,' he said.

She saw a brown envelope with his name on it as she passed the desk on her way to change. From it peeped a printed form that could have been a pathological report. She wondered idly what case that could be.

He was filling in another form to go with the specimens. 'Wash well,' he ordered all the staff. 'I want everyone to soak their hands in Sublimate or a similar solution before washing again and drying.' Orders were repeated in Italian and Theresa was amazed at the stern voice which would take no refusal lightly. A nurse brought a bowl of the blue liquid and the full precautions were taken. A growing fear struck the English girl as she washed the solution from her hands. Pietro saw the theatre nurse collecting swabs and told her to put them in a plastic sack for burning. Even said in Italian, the orders were clear to Theresa and she watched the linen go into a tub of disinfectant to soak until morning before being sluiced ready for the laundry.

'You've had the result of the test for TB,' she said. Pietro pretended not to hear. 'Your eyes! Have you sent a smear?'

He looked down at the anxious face, the quivering lips and the worried green eyes. 'It's worth being a patient to generate such concern in the beautiful breast of Nurse Callan,' he said, lightly. 'Tell me, do you look like that each time a result comes back?'

'Tell me,' she pleaded. 'Has the boy got tuberculosis?'

'Ah, I thought it was too good to expect such concern for me.' He bent and kissed her cheek. 'Thank you for caring about . . . the boy. Yes, I'm afraid the test was positive, and that's why I had to act quickly tonight.' He sealed the form into an envelope. 'The cultures haven't come back, but they had enough tissue to look at a section and there were TB bacilli.' He called to a nurse to take the specimen down to the hall ready for early collection. 'Let's get out of this place for coffee.' She changed with speed and joined him at the door. She turned to say goodbye to the staff there. 'Really goodbye?' he asked and she found that they were going to the lift leading to his quarters.

'Really goodbye,' she said, 'But I'm beginning to feel like a prima donna who says she is making her last appearance. I seem to have given several encores after making up my mind to go back to England.'

He switched on the light in the elegant hallway to his apartment and went in through the sitting-room to the kitchen. Theresa lingered in the doorway, unsure what to do. She no longer felt threatened—she had his word that he would not harass her in any way—but it didn't seem right to feel safe with him. She heard the water being drawn to fill the coffee machine and relaxed. Coffee would be good. The irregular hours of the past few days were catching up on her. The freshness after a nap in the afternoon had gone with the false elation of working at an absorbing case after midnight. She yawned and sat down in a deep armchair that enfolded her like a womb. It was cool and comfortable and only a faint soothing hum told of the sophisticated air-conditioning. Absentmindedly, she kicked off her shoes and snuggled down in the cushions.

Her hair was tied back in the pale green chiffon scarf that earlier had added to the effect of her dress but which now was tight and crumpled, securing the mass of auburn hair. She slid it from her head, shaking her hair free until it lay like a bronze filigree over the dark rose cushion. She was so comfortable and she hated the thought of venturing out into the night to take a water taxi back to the hotel . . .

'Theresa?' It was a voice she had heard so often in her dreams, and now she was dreaming again. Never in reality would his voice be so tender for her. For Francesca, it was soft and understanding, for Selina, warm and teasing, as if they were friends. She wrinkled her nose. Only friends? That had puzzled her when she was awake. The voice came again, 'Theresa . . . *amatissima* . . . *prediletta*,' words she didn't understand but which surely were endearments?

She stirred and opened her eyes. Pietro was standing before her with a tray of coffee cups and biscuits and cheese. He made a small movement that took him further from her chair. 'Don't sleep yet,' he said, gruffly. 'I can't keep the coffee hot for ever.'

'I wasn't asleep,' she protested.

'Only for half an hour,' he said. She sat up, pushing the hair from her eyes. 'Now, don't move quickly or you'll feel terrible.'

'I'm sorry. I had no idea. What a mess I must look.'

'Charming. But drink this and ask me to eat something before I starve.'

She smiled and held out the plate to him with exaggerated courtesy. 'You could have eaten them all and I would never have known,' she said, but she took a piece of cheese and nibbled it. 'I was only dozing,' she said, more to convince herself than Pietro.

'You didn't hear the phone?' he asked, taking another biscuit.

'The telephone?'

'The house phone. Our patient is breathing more regularly, is conscious and everything seems to be responding. They have the order of anti-TB drugs for use as soon as he can take them, but that is the least of his worries and ours. If he can build up his resistance, I think he'll do.'

Theresa felt ridiculously delighted, as if they shared something precious. 'I'm so glad,' she said. 'When I get back to England, I'd like to send him something . . . a get-well card in English to amuse him, or something like that.'

'You are going? Is it too late to make you change your mind?' He looked about him. 'This is a very comfortable apartment. You would be free to make it your home while you worked here. I don't know what I would have done tonight without your support.'

'That's silly. You managed very well before I came and your staff are very good.' She looked round the well-appointed room. 'I can't understand you. At the hotel, you make me feel like a prisoner and yet you would have much more gossip if you had me living here.'

'Let me show you the apartment.' He led her through to the kitchen, then the bathroom, and opened the door to his bedroom. The blue silk cover was flung back ready for occupation and the soft pillows looked inviting. Dark rose curtains of gauzy fabric fluttered in the breeze made by a fan and she could see a dressing-room opening from the master bedroom. She gasped. Was this the only bedroom? If it was, then the ritual of showing her the whole apartment was a declaration. It was saying that there was only one way that she could live there, with one man, with one bedroom, as one. She closed her eyes for a second, swaying slightly, but he was opening another door. Her reaction was relief mixed with something perilously like disappointment. The bed was single and co-vered with white lace. The dressing-table was very feminine and the room the prettiest she had seen outside a glossy magazine. She hoped that her gasp could be taken to mean that she was very impressed.

'A little frilly, but most women seem to like it,' he said. 'Francesca chose the cover and the curtains and Selina had a hand in the design of the fitments. A girl of many talents,' he added.

'So I noticed,' said Theresa, dryly. 'Now that I am awake and fed, I think I should be going back to the Danieli. Is it possible to have a taxi, or shall I walk? It isn't very far, is it?'

'It may not look far when you are on the water, but there are many bridges and detours to take if you walk.' He made no attempt to tell her about water taxis.

'May I get tidy?'

He stood back, letting her go into the bathroom. He handed her a clean towel from a pile on the side and shut the door as he left.

'I'll be in the sitting-room,' he called.

Theresa washed her face in cold water. Any romantic ideas she might have had vanished. So, Francesca was very familiar with the apartment and he had known Selina long enough to let her help to choose the fitments of the smaller bedroom. As she left the bathroom, Theresa glanced towards the main bedroom. The door was open and a suitcase was on the bed. She frowned. He had made no mention of going away, but she supposed that as he was living part of the time at the Danieli, he must bring cases of clothes between his two homes. The door of the wardrobe was open on either side, as if he had opened both doors in his rush to get at his own clothes. She stared. His clothes were still there, except for the dark suit and pile of shirts in the case, but the other side, where the rail of dresses had been, was empty. Her mouth was dry as she joined him in the sitting-room. Selina had cleared out everything, ready for the next occupant. 'I really ought to go,' she said.

Pietro smiled, but the warmth didn't reach his eyes. 'Yes, we ought to be on our way.'

'You are coming, too?'

'Of course. I couldn't let you go out alone at four in the morning.' He went into the bedroom, snapped shut the case and brought it out into the hall. 'I have to go away for a day or so,' he said. 'Can you wait for five more minutes while I telephone?'

She sat on a straight-backed chair while his voice rose and fell, but she understood nothing of what was said. He seemed almost anxious that she should go, and she began to think that he regretted his idea of her living in the apartment. Perhaps, even now, he was telephoning Selina, begging her to come back. She frowned. He was talking on the house phone, not taking an external call.

'Sorry if I kept you waiting,' he said. 'I had to arrange for Raphael to look after my patients while I'm away. Two things,' he said, briskly. 'I would like to let you know how George and the boy progress and Francesca wanted your address in London.' He handed her a piece of note paper on which she wrote her address and telephone num-

ber. He handed her a sealed envelope. 'For Mr
Nuttall if you see him before I do. No rush, but I'd
like him to have it before the end of the month.'

'I'll see that he gets it,' she said. 'I might do a
part-time job there for a few weeks before I go to
midwifery.'

He took her shoulders in his hands and looked
down into her face, sadly. 'Why there and not here,
Theresa? I need you here.'

'No, you have never needed me,' she said. 'I
would be useless with no Italian. I managed for
the odd case, but to train staff I need to be able to
talk to them. I am happier in my own hospital,
among—'

'Among your own people, away from these
lecherous Italians?'

'You won't let me forget that remark, will
you?'

'You have never let me forget it, Theresa.' He
kissed her gently on the cheeks and then briefly on
the mouth. 'You see, I can be the perfect English
gentleman.' His grip tightened. 'But we'll get that
taxi before I remember that I am Italian, too.' He
kissed her again, with hard dry kisses full of controlled passion. '*Andiama*,' he said, and opened
the door of the lift.

The water was lapping quietly in the dawn light
as they reached San Marco. The gilding shone with
molten light on the high pillars and the proud lions
faced the square, expecting invasion. Sleepy pigeons fanned out over their territories, too early for

the tourists who would feed them and stand before the clock tower to have photographs taken in the dazzling sunlight. 'I wish that I could come back as a tourist.' She said it without thinking and saw that he was annoyed.

'If you had stayed, I could have shown you Venice, the real Venice, away from the souvenir stands and the fake pottery.'

'I have glimpsed the real Venice and it threatens me,' she whispered. 'I should be safer with a bossy courier taking me round the city and out to the islands.'

'I could take you to Torcello before you go back.' He smiled. 'It was a famous, thriving island before Venice was born and has a softness that comes of history in decay. It also has charm and timelessness.'

'No, there isn't time.' She ached to stay with him, even if she would be just another woman in his life, to be used professionally as well as sexually—and if she stayed in his apartment, that would surely follow. 'I have my ticket.'

He put a finger to the corner of one eye and blinked. 'Are your eyes all right? I'll put in one more lot of drops before I go, if you like. Did you manage them alone?' For the last few instillations, he had waved her offers of help aside, saying that he had already done it.

'Yes, they're fine. I have some dust in the corner, that's all.' She was uneasy. A slight inflammation that could be due to a speck of dust made one eye slightly red. From his bleak expression, she knew that he wanted no further comment about his eyes, but she had to know.

'You will have a smear taken? It's only a wise precaution that you would make any of your staff take.'

'I'll do that if I think it is necessary,' he said. 'Here we are. I want a shower, some food and some rest.' She nodded. 'Meet you in the dining-room in half an hour?'

'Yes, that should be time enough.' She went back to her room but he stayed at Reception to telephone. It was ten minutes later that she heard him come back, just as she went to her room after her shower. She put aside the clothes she would wear while she was in Venice and packed the rest, quickly. If I rest for a few hours, I can wander about and say goodbye to the city I have yet to explore, she thought. In a few years, perhaps, I can come back and laugh about the feelings I have now. When I marry a nice solid citizen who will adore me and give me nice children, we shall come on holiday and stay at the Lido. A day trip to see the Doge's Palace and to the islands to buy lace and glass, and I shall have a wonderful time.

The tears that hovered, unshed, told her that she was a liar who would never dare to come back to a place with such memories of what might have been if she had been less scrupulous and more giving. Selina, with her easy relationships, was to be envied, but not followed. She closed the case as if it shut in the last of her emotions, and went downstairs to breakfast.

Pietro was already dressed in a formal suit, and his case and light raincoat were by the coat stand in the foyer.

'Are you going now?' she asked.

'I telephoned and I am wanted as soon as possible.' He gave a wry smile. 'So, even if you had accepted, the trip to Torcello is off. That is the story of my life. Would you mind ringing the Cipriani when you think that Francesca might be out of bed?' She nodded. 'Just to tell her that I shall be away for a few days and that George expects her for lunch today. He can sip cold soup while she has sea-food. Poor George, that will be torture for him.' He was trying to be lighthearted, but the going was rough.

'I'll tell her,' said Theresa. 'When she is married, she will have George to do her bidding. Can you give up that to him, easily?'

He stared at her. 'I think that, in England, the family hasn't the same strength as it has here. I can think of no time when I shall stop caring what happens to my dear cousin. I have known her for so long, helped her over a few awkward patches and, I suppose, spoiled her a little.' He laughed, more naturally. 'But you have to admit that she has charm, and I love her.'

'Your cousin?' Her picture of Francesca as a *femme fatale* crumbled.

He glanced at his watch and pushed his table

napkin on to the plate. 'Of course,' he said. 'What did you think she was? My mistress?' He laughed aloud. He came round to Theresa and bent to kiss her cheeks. '*Arrivederci, cara.*' He saw her stricken expression. 'I think that you might miss me a little,' he said. 'Wish me luck.' He strode away without looking back, leaving her to sort out her thoughts.

If Francesca was his cousin, his attitude to her was correct, affectionate and wholly commendable. 'Fool! How could I have been such a fool?' she said. She sipped more coffee, to steady her mind. How could she rush after him, crying that she had misjudged him? But it altered nothing. He had wanted her as he wanted Selina and nothing would convince her that Selina was a cousin.

She finished clearing the cupboard and drawers in her room, then wandered down to the Riva and walked along as far as the Maritime Museum. Holiday crowds took up more and more of the promenades as the day progressed, and she was glad to go back to the cool hotel for a light lunch. She rang Francesca who scolded her for leaving and seemed very curious about her future plans, asking quite bluntly if she was returning to a lover or to get married. 'I said that it was so,' she told Theresa, with satisfaction. 'Luigi said you had a lover or you would have been kinder to him, and Pietro told him that it showed that you had a rare virtue and taste to refuse him. They were quite heated,' said Francesca.

'I have to go back to work before this place

bewitches me completely,' said Theresa, lightly. 'I hope to see you when you come to England.'

'And Pietro?'

'We may meet again. We know the same people and I think we are going to a party given by a friend at St Edmund's.'

She walked away, limp with the heat and sleepy. A good rest, some food and an early night were what was needed or she would become weepy in this fabulous, heartless place.

Her room was cool and inviting, the only discordant note being the packed cases and the fresh clothes ready to wear to the airport in the morning. A place for loving, but not for a woman alone. In that, he had been right, so why had she refused the loving? She slept and then checked her tickets and papers, restlessly. She knew that she had packed everything but she seemed to be subconsciously aware that something was missing. She opened each drawer in turn, recalling the time when she had left a cardigan in the back of a drawer in a hotel in the Lake District.

The drawers were empty and the dress hangers were empty. It was only when the water taxi was on the way to the airport that she remembered the green dress.

It was too late to do anything about it. She had left enough time to check in at the airport but little to spare. It was much too hot to rush back to the apartment and if she did so, there was no possibility of getting into his rooms if he was away. She shrugged. Just as well it was gone. It would be a white elephant of a dress that she would have no opportunity of putting on for any of the parties to which she was likely to be invited.

The air crackled with information as the flights were called. Idly, she listened to a French voice alerting passengers for Paris and she saw the line of people at the check-in. A fair head seemed familiar and she craned her neck to see that it really was Selina. She seemed to be having trouble with the girl at the desk who was charging her for excess baggage. Two huge suitcases that seemed much too solid and utilitarian for such a glamorous creature to be taking as her luggage, stuck out of the weighing area. Selina shrugged and paid and then Theresa was borne along in the rush for her plane to Gatwick.

'Who am I fooling?' she asked the free airline magazine when she was settled by a window. Francesca may be his cousin, but those clothes would fit well into those huge cases. Selina obviously believed in taking all her perks when she left a lover, and who could blame her if she had given good value?

The mist over Giudecca hid the islands and the air hissed through the in-flo with irritating monotony. Theresa used the last of her Italian change to buy a drink and silently said a last and final goodbye to Venice.

CHAPTER NINE

'ARE you quite sure you want to come back?' Sister Pomery looked anxiously at Theresa. 'Heaven knows I can do with your help and the Senior Nursing Officer asked me to find a substitute for Nurse Benton while she is ill, but you really ought to have a holiday before you do midwifery. Have you any idea how hard you will work?'

'I went to Venice to nurse a man with heart disease and found that I was the mainstay of a theatre team on night duty! So this will seem a holiday compared with that one.'

'You look very fit,' Sister Pomery regarded her with interest. 'You haven't fallen in love, have you? Found a dashing gondolier? There's a certain bloom that suggests something like that. Sad, though,' she added with her usual bluntness. 'Didn't come up to scratch? Strange, when I think of the usual passionate latin lover.'

'Don't mention latin lovers.' It was a relief to tell her about Luigi's amorous advances and to make that the explanation of her lack of enthusiasm for Italians. Sister Pomery chuckled. 'And if Mr Nuttall asks about my time in Venice, please don't say anything bad about the men there. The last time I scrubbed for him here, the assistant was a man who

171

took a very dim view of my opinion of his countrymen.'

'The gorgeous Peter Bassano? I was forgetting.
He was in Venice. I hope you didn't come to blows
when you met again.'

'Not exactly, but he doesn't have a very high
opinion of me, except as a nurse. He wanted me to
stay in his theatre for keeps.'

'Lucky you. Why *did* you come back, Callan?'

'It was a live-in job which could have become
rather complicated.'

'Nice complications,' said Pomery and unlocked
the drug cupboard to get out a new supply of heart
stimulants to be ready for the afternoon list. 'He
caused quite a stir among our young virgins.'

'He does seem to attract women,' said Theresa in
a level voice, 'but I didn't like the idea of being one
of a crowd.'

'Pity. It's funny, I never thought of him as a
Casanova. He treated everyone here very correctly, to the point of chill.'

'In England, he is English, but in Italy, the other
parent's influence comes into play.' She sighed.
'Even I feel different. In the hot sun with all that
colour, I felt on the brink of an adventure that
never happened, but here, I can get excited about a
trip to the cinema!'

'Well, if you really intend working here for
another three weeks, you can start tomorrow. Nothing very complicated but a fairly long list, mostly
bronchoscopies.'

Theresa went across to the room allotted to her and unpacked. She had brought only a few things from her flat in London and could go back there again at the weekend to change her clothes and fill in the gaps of her temporary wardrobe. It was good to be back, she told herself, and wise to have come to St Edmund's at once, before she lapsed into a lazy round of doing very little more than being sorry for herself. She found the tiny pink elephants that had been made on the island of Murano and smiled, wistfully. To think of Pietro Bassano as anything but a surgeon and the lover of another woman was madness—and as unreal as seeing pink elephants!

The park was bright with newly rainwashed grass and she borrowed a pair of rubber boots and the shaggy dog belonging to the kitchen superintendent who was pleased to have someone to exercise her. 'Come on, Minnie,' she called and walked quickly up the hill to the lane leading to a wide grassy plain. She breathed in the fresh air and the scents of the flowers. It was better here than in the heavy electric atmosphere of Venice on the edge of a sirocco, but she missed the noise and laughter, the beauty of the buildings and the faces of the people. She thrust her hands deep into her pockets and looked at the sky line. Minnie chased imaginary rabbits and came back panting.

George would be sitting out, now, with Francesca hovering over him, loving him and spoiling him. The boy with the tubercular abscess must be better, too. Would he be able to work on the fruit boats again, selling richly purple aubergines, bright oranges and woodland strawberries, and, of course, peaches? A tendency to clear her throat made her wonder if she had taken cold. It couldn't be homesickness for a city she had lived in for such a short time. I'm spoiled by living in a beautiful hotel among cultured people, she decided. It has nothing to do with life in a real sense, it just has a lingering poignancy as one has from a good holiday that comes to an end.

What had she to face? A long list tomorrow that would be exhausting but boring. She might ring up a couple of friends and go to a theatre one evening, or she might go swimming in the local baths. Big deal. There would be the party before she went to Charlotte's—that was quite soon now. She called to the dog and began to descend the rough path. What to wear, now that her dress had disappeared? Perhaps Selina had taken it to make up the numbers of her own dresses when she found the silk one gone. It wasn't important. That dress would do very well and if Pietro Bassano came to the party, he would know that it hadn't been wasted on her. She could think of no partner to take to the party, although Mr Nuttall encouraged staff to bring boyfriends to his occasions.

The hospital lay before her, in the hollow at the bottom of the hill. Built during the last war, it was an uneasy compromise between solid stone structures and single storey buildings added for extra ward space and never replaced by more permanent ones. There were many trees and a large kitchen garden manned by patients in the long-stay wards for the handicapped. It all looked green and well-ordered and the children from the ward at the end of a block had their own play area and lawn. Several toddlers in plaster were playing in a sand pit, looking like tiny dolls from that distance. I ought to be happy here, thought Theresa. I wept at the thought of leaving, yet now I feel as if I am a stranger.

She squinted against the sun. In the car park, the cars were moving. She saw a man push a large case into a boot and slam the door down. That would be Mr Burton, the orthopaedic surgeon, on his way from one list to his private patients. The surgical lists and clinics would be closing, one by one. What day of the week was it? Orthopaedics and allergies this afternoon, and in the other clinic, eyes and ENT. There was Mr Caldwell, the eye surgeon. She smiled. Even at this distance, there was no mistaking him. He walked rather like a crab and rumour had it that he had refused an operation to straighten one foot, but the result was a very characteristic walk. He had another man with him. Could that be his new house surgeon? It was impossible to see faces from that distance, but the man lacked the white coat and subservient manner of someone being given orders about patients.

This man stood tall and walked with fluid grace, an equal or a superior with the man who led the country in his skill as an eye surgeon. Theresa threw a stick for the dog and ran after her. How stupid to think that any man with broad shoulders and thick dark hair must be Pietro Bassano. What would he be doing here? A list of routine broncho-scopies and one dilation of pylorus wouldn't bring him from Venice, and what would he have to say to a surgeon from another team? Eyes were far removed from chest and heart surgery.

She stopped so suddenly that she slid on the wet grass and floundered in the muddy verge of the lane. Oh, no! She had a picture of Pietro Bassano with a slightly red eye which he rubbed as if it irritated. He must have come to consult the surgeon because the results of the tests were positive and he was now having a reaction to the diseased tissue coughed into his face during the bronchoscopy.

She walked down slowly. What happened when an eye was infected with the baccillus? Whatever it was must be bad to have forced theatre staff to have the rule about immediate irrigation of eyes exposed to risk. The lane wound round between hedges that now hid the hospital and when she reached the road the car park was nearly empty. There was no sign of either of the two men, and she had no way of finding out what was happening. She returned to the kitchens one damp dog, and accepted a slab of cake with sultanas for her tea.

The admissions clerk looked up in surprise, as Theresa wandered into the records department.

The girl looked at the clock, pointedly.

'I won't keep you. I wanted to know if any member of staff had been admitted for treatment?'

'Thought you'd left. No, only the nurse from theatre and that wasn't today. Who had you in mind?'

'I heard a rumour that one of the visiting surgeons was here for treatment,' Theresa lied.

'News to me, and if it's true, I don't want to know tonight. I'm off now and if that phone rings, I'm not answering it.' She looked at Theresa, willing her to leave so that she could lock her department.

At least he isn't warded, and it might not have been him, Theresa thought brushing the wet earth from her skirt as she went to her room. She could write to Francesca, or ring the clinic in Venice. No, not that. If she rang, it would suggest undue concern about someone she had met for such a short time and they might not know any details if he had left them without telling anyone about his plans.

Did even Francesca know what he was doing? He was fond of her and unlikely to worry her until he was sure of anything wrong. She recalled Selina, struggling with the cases full of clothes. She might know more than anyone. She had flown to Paris for a day or so. Might she not be coming over to London after that visit? If he was in England, they would meet and probably continue the relationship that meant so little to either of them but satisfied their baser needs.

The evening seemed endless and Theresa went

over to the main block to listen to music and to read, hoping to find one of her old friends to talk to. She found a pile of nearly new magazines and settled down to look at them. A centre spread caught her eye. Selina, smiling in the seductive manner that Theresa knew so well, was leaning against a pillar. She looked more closely. It was one of the pillars in the Piazzetta by San Marco. The caption read: 'Danger for men who venture here, more deadly than in the time of the Doges.' Selina had a background of girls clutching the arms of men who seemed to be struggling rather half-heartedly between the two pillars that had been used as a place of execution in medieval times.

The dress was one that Theresa had last seen on the rail in the cupboard at the luxurious penthouse apartment. She flicked over the page, and there was Selina wearing the pure silk turquoise dress that Pietro had casually given her to wear after the operation. The huge hat was incidental to the scene in Florian's café, and the pigeons walked solemnly by the table. The next showed Selina again, with two more matronly models, smartly dressed, but in less way-out colours, and Theresa realised that she was looking at the collection of clothes kept in the cupboard in Venice.

'Lovely face,' said a nurse, coming up behind her. 'What a life. Swans about to all the capitals of Europe wearing beautiful clothes. They are in London next week at the Savoy, wearing the same collection.'

'She's a model! She really is a model.'

The nurse looked at her curiously. 'Top model, and she has a share in a clothes design business, with a chain of shops. Not often you get a beauty with good business sense.'

'I met her in Venice,' said Theresa, to account for her rising colour.

'How exciting.'

'It could have been,' said Theresa, smiling to hide her deep despair. 'It could have been quite thrilling, but I didn't know she was a model. But I did know someone who let her use space to store her clothes.'

She pretended to read, but the pictures haunted her. So many incidents that she had not interpreted correctly came to her tortured mind. Only her reaction to Luigi now seemed valid—he was an attractive snake. She had misjudged all the others and Pietro Bassano had every right to think she was a mindless, frigid little prude who shied away from men like a frightened pony. Selina smiled up from the pages with fun-loving eyes, amoral but honest in her capacity to give. And now it was too late even to ask if Pietro was all right. How could she telephone? What would he think of her?

She flung the magazines on the table and went to her room. If he had been to see the eye-man, the nurses there would know. She no longer cared if they thought she was running after a man who despised her. In the dining-room, she took a salad and asked if Mr Caldwell was working in Out-patients that day. 'In eyes,' she said.

Nurse Welsh nodded. 'He had a lovely-looking man there with him.'

'Helping?'

'No, for examination.' Theresa felt her colour slipping away. 'Are you all right?'

'Yes. Was it Mr Bassano? I was with him when some tubercular discharge went into his eyes.'

'Oh, it was you, was it?' The girl smiled as if something amused her very much. 'Have a good time in Venice?'

'Not very. How is he?'

'He sent over a smear which someone did badly. Wasn't you, I hope.' She looked stern. 'We are taught to do it so that we can't possibly scratch the eyes with the loop, but whoever did his scraped the cornea.' Theresa caught her breath and assured Nurse Welsh that she had no idea he had had a smear taken. 'Just as well if you're thinking of coming back here. You'd never have lived it down. If the eyes had been infected, I don't know what damage could have been caused if there was a raw spot ready to absorb more bacilli.'

'You said "if". Does that mean the tests are clear?'

'Quite clear. He said he discontinued his drops and made sure that the eye had no antibiotics before he asked a friend to take the specimen.' She sniffed. 'Some ham-handed friend.'

'Thank you,' said Theresa, almost speechless

with joy. 'Thank you.' She dashed away, leaving her supper untouched. It didn't matter that he would never be more to her than a colleague, it didn't matter so much that he would never seek her out to talk to her, to be with her, to make love to her. His eyes were all right and her fears were gone. It no longer mattered that the other nurses thought that Venice had turned her brain. She was happy for him, even if her own heart was broken.

She prepared uniform for the morning, using the white dress she had had in Venice as she had given in all her St Edmund's clothes and would use her own until she did midwifery. The good finish from the laundry used by the Danieli Hotel in Venice still remained and a touch with a cool iron made the dress crisp and neat. She polished the buckle of her belt and made up a tiny cap. When she saw the uniform hanging on the wardrobe door when she woke from a restless night, she thought that, once more, she was in the suite at the Danieli.

The patter of rain against the window soon dispelled such thoughts and she hurried over to breakfast, trying to think of the work to be done. When the sun refused to shine all that day, the main steriliser broke down and the drug basket was late in the theatre, she wished that she was back in Venice, even if she would have to wander about alone there.

The lists during the next few days were long and she now knew why they were busy. One of the wards was open again after re-decorating, so that all the beds were ready for fresh faces and conditions due in theatre. She was busier than she had been for months and tired enough to sleep as soon as she tumbled into bed at night. Life will be like this, she thought. Painless but somehow pointless.

'You know it's the party tonight,' said Mr Nuttall when he popped in to make sure that his registrar needed no advice. He had been away for a few days explaining a new technique and reading a medical paper at a university. He looked round the theatre until he saw Theresa. 'Hello, heard you were back. The party is at eight, but I want you there at seven-thirty. Want a word,' he said, and hurried out again.

'I expect he wants you to give up your day off to help him with his private aortic valve,' said the registrar.

'His valve? I thought he looked very well,' said Theresa, hiding her consternation at his words.

'Funny girl,' said the registrar. 'You don't think he wants your body, do you?'

'He might,' she replied. 'There are them that does!' It was easy to joke as if she was happy and free of hang-ups.

'Not our very-married boss.'

'No, not him.' She cleared away from the last case. Her hair was lank with steam and her face was hot and pink. 'I feel like going to bed. I think I'll miss the party,' she said to Sister Pomery.

'Don't be silly. You've worked much too hard

since you came back. Have fun. He is a very
generous host and his parties are memorable. If
you go to Charlotte's, you will have to be on duty
for long periods and you'll be exhausted.'

'Fun? To be asked to give up even more off-duty
to help with a case? That's all men want from me.'

'That I do not believe,' Sister laughed. 'A hot
bath, and dressed up, and you'll feel better. Mr
Nuttall is sending a car for you as he wants to talk to
you first.'

'So it is something serious?'

'He said it was vital, but you know what he is. He
thinks everything he does is important.'

'In that case, I'd better get going.' Theresa had
no time to wonder who would be there. If Pietro
Bassano arrived, he would be busy with girls who
smiled at him and treated him as if he were a god.
He would have no time for her now, and if Mr
Nuttall wanted to talk shop, then she would be
avoided by any attractive doctors who didn't want
to be dragged into extra duties with the keen
surgeon.

She bathed and washed her hair, drying it fast so
that it was really much fluffier than she liked it. I
really do look like a doll, as that nice American
said. Why aren't all men like Hugo, she thought,
then made a face. Rather none than a warm syrup
of love twenty-four hours a day. How contrary can I
get?

As she left the bathroom, she saw a nurse leave a
parcel at the door. When she opened it, she found

her pleated dress, with a note from Selina apologising for taking it with her other models. 'I counted the garments and found the numbers right, then had a message that Pietro had bought one of the collection. I hope you don't mind. I wore the dress for a show and we are contacting the designer to do some for us. It's very pretty.'

There was no postmark, no address other than her name, so it must have been delivered by hand. She must be in England now, visiting friends, doing the fashion show or seeing Pietro. Undecided what to wear, Theresa held the dress in front of her. The touch of it evoked memories of the evening in the Cipriani and the bizarre trip in evening dress to the operating theatre. She put it on the bed and began to make up her eyes. A tap on the door made her start. It was almost as if Luigi might walk in with a tray of drinks and an amorous look in his eyes. But this was England, and, more than that, this was a flat for nurses and there was no danger of wandering men among the few doctors living in the building.

The corridor was empty, and Theresa thought that she had imagined the sound. She looked down and nearly stepped on the box that lay at her feet. It was a cardboard box with a window front, showing one perfect orchid of a colour that matched the dull green of the pleated dress and would tone with the bronze make-up she used with it. There was no note, but her heart beat faster. She knew that Pietro was in the building as surely as if he stood there holding the orchid for her to pin on the dress.

Five minutes and the car would be there for her. She adjusted the narrow straps that held her feet in the slender high-heeled sandals and picked up her bag and the light coat more suitable for an English evening than the gossamer shawl she had worn in Venice. She saw the car through the frosted glass of the front door and the shape of the driver, standing ready to help her in.

Pietro smiled. 'We both made it,' he said. 'I was afraid that the dress was lost, but Selina looked after it well.' He regarded her with tender affection, as if there had never been a harsh word exchanged. 'Francesca said to thank you for writing to her and she will be in touch.' Was that the reason why he was so relaxed with her? Anything she did for Francesca would please him. A tinge of jealousy made her hurry to the car. 'Are we catching a bus?' he said, reminding her of the time when she had said that to him.

'Mr Nuttall asked me to get there half an hour early.'

'I know. I asked him to tell you.'

'You did?'

'Of course. Once we are talking to other people, I shall have so little time alone with you, Theresa.'

He drove swiftly past the lane leading to the down and the new roadhouse where the party was to be. 'You missed the turning,' she said.

'No, we can go back soon, but first we have things to say.' He stopped the car overlooking a slope of green with sparse trees edging a small stream, and switched off the engine.

'I think we ought to go,' she said, in a low voice. I've steeled my heart to resist you, she thought, but here, under paler skies, you are different. His dark eyes were the same, only gentler, lacking the arrogance she'd seen in Venice. His hands were gentle as he took both of hers and turned her to face him. 'Tell me what you think of me,' he said. Was this the vanity of a man used to praise? She glanced up and saw that his face was pale, as if the answer was of great importance. 'You thought that Francesca, my dear, spoiled little cousin, was my mistress?' She nodded. 'You then thought that I had so little consideration for my future wife that I would sleep with Selina, of all people!'

It was almost a relief to hear the offended dignity and a tiny smile began to form. 'Everything told me that this was true,' she said, 'And Luigi did nothing to convince me that Italian men were better than I had imagined.'

'Luigi is a pain in the neck,' he said, forcibly.

She laughed. 'You sound so English,' she said. 'In Venice, you would never use that expression.'

'I have to be so here, or you will run away like that small rabbit running over the grass.' He kissed her cheek and laughed, softly. 'You know I want you badly, darling.' He felt her stiffen as she dreaded his next words, the softening up towards seduction. 'I also happen to love you very much, but you will never let me get to that word.'

'If you used that first, it might help,' she said, softly, knowing that if he loved her, she would be his for ever, under any conditions.

'Little fool,' he said, tenderly. 'Why do you think I was so anxious that your good name should be unsullied? Why did I follow you wherever you went, making sure that you were at no risk?' She saw that his eyes were not laughing, but full of a great and deep emotion that had nothing to do with casual liaisons. 'It matters,' he said, simply. 'These things do matter, even if our friends tell us that we should take love where we find it. I want you for my own.' He kissed her and her heart fluttered wildly. Her arms were round his neck and his face buried in the softness of her breast. He murmured endearments in English and Italian and she knew that she had won both the men in that wonderful body and mind.

It was Pietro who put her from him, his hands reluctant, but with firm gentleness.

'Darling,' she breathed. 'Darling, Peter.'

'Peter in England, and here I can observe the conventions more easily.' He kissed her once more. 'Now, we go to the party and tell everyone that we are to be married.'

'So soon?'

'Can you wait?' She blushed. 'I am glad to know you can't. We can marry here, and you can say goodbye to this place, your relatives and the thought of other people's babies.'

'I forgot. I'm booked for midwifery training.'

'In such a prestigious school, they will have a dozen eager candidates willing to take your place.'

'I suppose so.' She looked at him in wonder. Was this really happening to her? 'And after? Where are you taking me?' The fire in her veins made her gasp with pleasure as his hands caressed her and his lips sought hers again.

'We go to Venice to make love. There, I am Pietro, and you will know what passion I can teach you.'

She unpinned the crushed orchid from her dress. Not even that beauty must come between them. She closed her eyes, seeing again the vast bed with the heavy silk cover and knew that it would be home.

The romantic gift for Christmas

First time in paperback, four superb romances by favourite authors, in an attractive special gift pack. A superb present to give. And to receive.

United Kingdom £3.80
Publication 14th October 1983

Darkness of the Heart
Charlotte Lamb

Virtuous Lady
Madeleine Ker

Trust in Summer Madness
Carole Mortimer

Man-Hater
Penny Jordan

Look for this gift pack where you buy Mills & Boon romances

Doctor Nurse Romances

Amongst the intense emotional pressures of modern medical life, doctors and nurses often find romance. Read about their lives and loves in the other three Doctor Nurse titles available this month.

SURGEON IN DANGER
by Kate Ashton

In the five years since she last saw Dr David Duncan, Claire Brown has learnt to forget the past in her vital work as sister on a Renal Unit. But when David reappears in her life can she come to terms with the fact that he is no longer the man she had known and loved?

IN THE NAME OF LOVE
by Hazel Fisher

'Stop antagonising Dr Alexandre,' Student Nurse Anna Curtis is told. But is it Anna's fault that her mere presence has such an adverse effect on the normally good-humoured senior surgical registrar?

DEAR DOCTOR MARCUS
by Barbara Perkins

Sisters dote on surgeon Marcus Tate, and staff nurses swoon. Even his private secretary, Carolyn Burne, is in danger of losing her heart. But can she once again bear to risk losing the man she loves to her glamorous sister?

Mills & Boon
the rose of romance